STEVEN LEA

Out Of His Depth

For Ed, for making me love books.

Acknowledgement

Thanks to my proof-readers, Fiona, Mary & Lea.

I

Prologue

Most people are right-handed, so before rudders were fitted to the back end of a boat, someone with a 'steer board' would sit on the right-hand side of the vessel to guide it along.
To avoid damage to the steerboard, the boat would dock with its left-hand side facing the port.

Chapter 1

I never expected to become a killer. But ever since that day I knew that I could. After what they did. It's not like I have a choice. It's all I can think about.

He's brought them all together for me. They weren't to blame, but they will help me get to the ones that are. They can help me change my future. Get back my life. I'll never get a chance like this again.

The first few need to look like accidents. Just until we're far enough away from civilisation that it doesn't matter anymore. Nobody will be able to help them then.

II

DAY ONE: SOUTHAMPTON

Chapter 2

Galaxy Cruise line's newest ship, Starlight, didn't follow the trend of bigger-is-better when she was launched from the Fincantieri shipyard in Italy just over a year ago. With 3500 passengers, 1500 crew, and weighing in at 115,000 tonnes, she is still an impressive sight at the quayside. Unlike some of her larger 'rivals' designed to appeal to the mass market and squeeze in almost 6000 passengers, Starlight was designed to be a modern update of the classic cruise liner – very elegant but modern design, décor and facilities, keeping away from chintz and definitely avoiding tacky. A mostly white outer hull with a few flashes of dark blue on the bow kept the outside tasteful, but inside the décor was smart, bordering on glitzy, as was the dress-code most evenings. Traditional dark wood furnishings and panelling were lifted by lots of chrome, silver, gold and crystal, clever lighting and luxurious colourful carpets. All of this, as with any cruise ship's interior, helped define Galaxy's ideal clients: welcoming to anyone, but perfect for a certain few.

Launched in early spring, and having just completed her first summer season in the Mediterranean, Starlight was now on her way to the Caribbean, whose 'winter' weather is usually as good if not better than summer in Europe. The journey west through the Med' and across the Atlantic was what some would call a repositioning cruise, calling at a few European ports before heading across the Atlantic in seven or eight days.

The ship's crew came from all over the world, mostly the Philippines and South America, Asia and Eastern Europe. They had been working hard throughout the night as the ship docked quietly in its home port, cleaning the public areas of the ship while the guests were sleeping, and then their staterooms later in the morning when they had disembarked.

A wet, grey November morning in Southampton isn't the most exotic place to begin a Caribbean cruise, but it is a good place for people looking for some winter sun to find a cruise ship heading south.

In principle, boarding a cruise ship is like catching a plane, only much more civilised. You check-in your luggage first, like at an airport, but you don't have to stand for hours in a queue – porters are only too keen to take your labelled suitcases from you when you arrive at the terminal and the next time you see them will be in your room a few hours later, getting ready for dinner. Lounges can be busy but arrivals are staggered to minimise queueing to have your passport checked, your hand luggage scanned, and receive the key that opens your stateroom door. Some older ships still use the hotel-style cards but Galaxy has the Sea Star, a metallic disc like a medium-sized coin, with your own star sign etched in silver on an enamel background of varying colours depending on your loyalty level. The Sea Star is the latest in wearable technology, fits in a wristband, bracelet, necklace, etc., and links to an app that allows passengers to keep tabs on each other, book seats for performances and order drinks from the bar to be delivered to wherever they happen to be lounging.

By mid-afternoon, more than three thousand passengers have walked along the gangways, passed through a large door in the side of the ship onto Deck Four and been greeted by immaculately-presented, smiling staff, given a glass of Prosecco or Champagne, and shown to a restaurant to find their first meal, the Lido Deck to find a sun lounger or hot tub, or one of the large public areas like the huge, circular, multi-storey Atrium inside the centre of the ship, where first-time cruisers stand at the railings overlooking three or four decks of bars, cafes, shops, lifts, and a dance floor at the lower level.

By 4 p.m. Starlight's bridge had made all the checks necessary for leaving the port. Doors were closed, ropes were untied and the ship slowly slipped out of the harbour into the Solent and turned southwest towards the Bay of Biscay, where it would sail south through the roughest part of the cruise. By the time the ship arrived in Lisbon three days later, the passengers would be well acclimatised to their home for the next two weeks.

III

DAY FOUR: LISBON

Chapter 3

After having the morning off to wander the streets of Portugal's capital city along with the majority of Starlight's passengers, Lucy Jones finished singing the last song of her first evening set in the Atrium and soaked up the applause from all around. A handful of couples on the twenty metre circular dance floor on Deck Five in front of her clapped politely and headed back to their places among the fifty or so seats scattered around the perimeter. There were no other empty ones and many people stood behind watching and sipping wine and cocktails before going for dinner.

The stage was set between two elaborately decorated glass elevator shafts that rose up through Decks Six, Seven and Eight. Lucy looked up and saw people ringing the balconies on each deck looking down at her and applauding her performance. Many were stood on the glass, gold and marble staircases that spiralled down, deck-by-deck, on either side of the vast space.

There was a buzz in the air this evening, as the guests had been ashore for the first time and had lots to talk about. Lucy was often reminded how lucky she was to have a job she loved at times like this. She stepped off the stage, thanked her backing musicians, and made her way graciously and gratefully through the audience, accepting their compliments, shaking hands, pressing the flesh. As much a part of being an entertainer as belting out the blues or whatever she turned her talents to.

Lucy walked through the Atrium, but then sneaked through 'crew only' doors and corridors to avoid any over-enthusiastic fans following, and emerged a few doors away from her own stateroom.

At 31, Lucy was in her prime-earning years in her industry. She was trained, talented, attractive and, she thought, ambitious, but had never quite got the break she dreamed of. Working on a cruise ship was a good way to earn a steady living as an entertainer, better than many would achieve, so she was grateful and worked hard, making three or four appearances a day, every day.

As she stood in front of the door to her room, she opened the small blue-sequinned clutch handbag she'd hidden under the piano on stage, which matched her strapless cocktail dress, took out her Sea Star bracelet and waved it at the door lock. It flashed green and she pushed the handle down and stepped inside.

On her left was a small bathroom where she'd soon be heading for a shower, on her right the wardrobes where she kept the racks of dresses and outfits for her job, plus some casual clothes and bikinis for occasional time in port and on deck. She walked past both towards the dressing table at the end of the wardrobes, kicked off her shoes and put her bag down. As she turned back towards the bathroom she glanced out of the small round window at the darkening evening outside. Facing toward the door again, she froze, straightened and her heart boomed in her chest as she stopped breathing and spun around.

"Shit! Michael! What the hell do you think you're doing!" she shouted at the half-naked man lying just about under the covers of her bed at the far end of the room. "You scared me to death. What the hell are you doing here?"

"Language, Lucy," said Michael, calmly.

"What do you expect when you break into my room? How did you get in here?" said Lucy, noticing his officer's uniform draped over a chair. Her heart was beating at twice its normal rate.

"I thought you'd be pleased to see me. You were always happy to see me the last time we were on the same ship. You knew I'd be here."

"That was just a bit of fun," Lucy said, looking away.

"It *was* fun," Michael replied, "You enjoyed it as much as I did."

Lucy took a deep breath to steady herself. Her heart began to slow back down but her face was flushed with the shock. She turned back towards the dresser and took off her jewellery, facing away from the bed. Yes, she had enjoyed herself when she'd last seen Michael, but didn't really want to admit it right now. Annoyed that he'd let himself in and scared her, she ignored him, stepped sideways and slid open a wardrobe door.

Lucy reached around her back and unzipped her dress as far as she needed to let it slip off and down over her hips so she could step out of it and grabbed a hanger. She put the loops in the dress into the wooden hanger's grooves and hung the dress in the wardrobe, standing slightly breathless in her underwear, pausing trying to compose herself. She caught her breath suddenly as she felt Michael's hands on her hips as he pulled her towards him, breathing gently into her ear.

Lucy turned slowly around in his arms, succumbing to his

15

warmth, his smell. His tall muscular body was a woman's fantasy and didn't he know it. She knew she wasn't the only one. She'd seen the way other female crew had smiled knowingly at him. Right now though he was hers if she wanted him.

Chapter 4

Mrs Margaret Gibson enjoyed her evening meal in Starlight's Four Seasons restaurant. Long retired, she was travelling on her own this time due to her husband's business commitments, she'd found herself on a table of ten with passengers from all over the world. Most were middle-aged Europeans, with a Scottish couple in their late twenties, a single South-American woman in her thirties and two gay American men. Conversation had certainly not been a problem. All but Margaret were cruising novices so she had plenty of tales to tell and opinions to share. As a veteran she was able to share her experiences of other ships and ports around the world with the newcomers.

The split level dining room sparkled from every mirror and light fitting scattered across the walls and ceilings. The dark wood furniture and red and black-patterned carpets gave the room a more formal atmosphere than the Atrium, but the volume was high as the guests talked excitedly about their plans for the trip. The staff moved about swiftly, bringing the food to the tables still hot, the sommeliers keeping everyone's glass filled. As it was the first formal night of the cruise, the gentlemen were in black ties and dinner jackets, and the ladies in cocktail dresses and evening gowns.

The food was some of the best Margaret had experienced in the sixteen cruises she'd been on, especially the lamb main course, cooked to perfection. A mediocre starter was made up for by a perfect crème Brulee dessert. A nibble of cheese and biscuits and a small cup of coffee would finish it off perfectly.

As the conversations bounced to-and-fro around the table, Margaret took a moment to sit back and take in her surroundings, to think how her husband would have enjoyed this new ship and the voyage across the Atlantic. She wiped her mouth with the corner of her napkin and put it down on the table in front of her, closed her eyes, let out a deep breath and slumped gently to her left side, cracking her temple against the top of the chair-back next to her, and fell to the floor.

Chapter 5

She had to go first.

A frail old woman she may have been but that will have some impact. I might even get two for the price of one. Her husband's heart is weak.

And it was easy. It doesn't take much to push an eighty-one-year-old off her mortal coil. So little as to be untraceable in fact. No one will suspect anything. Except for a dodgy meal. The chef will be questioned. The kitchens might be shut down and scrubbed. If they open her up they'll just find she died of heart failure. But we'll be long gone by then.

IV

DAY FIVE: GIBRALTAR

Chapter 6

"You need to find a woman," Rob said. At least that's what John Barker thought he'd heard as his eyes struggled to get used to the bright light from the screen of his cell phone in the darkness of his bedroom.

"What?" replied Barker, wishing he'd remembered to turn the damn thing off. Old habits die hard.

"You need to find a woman."

"Not funny Rob."

"I'm not being funny."

"My wife's been gone barely six months Rob, and why the hell are you ringing in the middle of the night?"

"Because I need you to find a woman for me. Urgently." Rob replied

"Rob, I don't need a woman and I certainly don't need to find you one. Are you drunk?" John was waking up but getting more irritated. "Ring me back in the morning when you've sobered up."

Rob persisted. "No John, I need you to go now and look for a specific woman. You said you'd help me if I needed anything in your neck of the woods. I never thought it would happen but it has."

"I didn't mean it Rob. It's what people say to their colleagues when they leave a job."

"But I need your help John."

"I left Rob, as far as I'm concerned. Permanently."

"Interpol has been onto us John. There's a woman that's popped up, supposed to have been dead a couple of years and they want to keep an eye on her. She's near you."

"I'm in Spain Rob, how near can she be?"

"She's on a ship," Rob replied, waiting for the reaction.

"A ship? She 'popped up' on a ship? How am I supposed to watch her on a ship? With binoculars?" Barker sat up on the edge of his bed, still confused and impatient. "What sort of ship?"

"A cruise ship John. You're going on holiday," Rob came back.

"A what? No I'm not. A cruise ship? No way."

"Oh come on John, it's the most luxurious stakeout you'll ever do in your life. All you've got to do is wander the ship for a week or so and keep an eye out for her."

Barker was out of bed now and on his way to the kitchen for a drink, "And how do I pick out one woman on a ship with thousands of people on board?"

"She's younger than the average passenger John, barely forty we think. Less than ten percent are that age, and half of those are men. So we've narrowed it down by ninety-five percent already. How easy do you want it?"

Barker sighed to himself without letting Rob hear it. He'd been coming to terms with the death of his wife for months and been on his own most of the time. He didn't feel ready to take on the world again yet but realised he wasn't going to sort his life out sat in a Spanish villa by himself reading and watching TV. He probably ought to take the job just to get out of the house.

"I don't have the right clothes here Rob. Don't you need posh clothes for a cruise? I don't have time to go shopping. And how do I get on it?"

"All taken care of John. Your bag is packed."

"What do you mean my bag is packed?" Barker asked suspiciously, dropping the plastic bottle of milk he'd retrieved from the fridge door shelf. "Shit!"

"I mean I've known you long enough to know roughly what size you are, so I got our contact near you to go shopping on your behalf and bring it to you. It's in the car." Rob explained.

"The car? Contacts?"

"Yes. There's a car on its way now. Be with you in an hour or so. Seville police department. He's going to pick you up and take you to Gibraltar to rendezvous with the ship in the morning."

"Jesus, you've been busy. I suppose you've picked me out a couple of ties too."

"Obviously," said Rob. "Your passport is still current isn't it?"

Barker paused for a second, realising he had a get-out if he wanted it. All he had to do was tell a white lie and say 'No, Rob, it expired last month,' or 'I lost it Rob,' and he couldn't go. But he couldn't bring himself to lie to Rob. They'd always been straight with each other when they'd worked together in the Met police for seven years. They'd never let each other down.

"Yes Rob," said Barker, this time letting him hear his sigh of resignation.

"Oh, and some sun cream," said Rob. "Don't forget that. You'll need it."

Chapter 7

"Senor Barker?" The officer said as he wound down his car window outside the small wrought iron gate at the entrance to Barker's villa, as dawn began to break.

"Ola. Si," said Barker, having found his passport and packed a few essentials, including sunblock, into a small sports bag in the hour since being woken by Rob's phone call. He threw the bag onto the back seat of the car and stood and went through a mental list of what he had packed, "I'll just turn the lights off and lock the doors," he said as wandered back, just giving himself another moment to take in what was going on.

"Ok Senor, we will be there in about two hours, maybe a little less," the uniformed man said as Barker walked back and climbed into the passenger seat next to him.

"Any instructions for me?" asked Barker.

"No sir, I was not told anything about the purpose of your visit to the port, except to say that Mr Johnson said he will email you the details. He suggested you download onto your phone the information before you get on board the ship."

Barker swiped his phone screen as the driver rolled quietly away from his house and towards the main road. Sure enough, there were a couple of emails from Rob, sent about half an hour ago. One with a PDF attached which he downloaded for reading later rather than try to read now in a moving car in the half-light. The other had a couple of pictures attached, presumably of the woman he was supposed to look for. They weren't the greatest photographs ever, taken from a distance into a crowd. But there seemed to be one or two of the same people in both shots, one male, one female. Again, he decided to look closer later and downloaded them into the photo gallery.

As the car turned left onto the main highway and picked up speed, he watched his villa disappear in the mirror and thought about his wife Laura. Maybe this was the first step into the new life he knew he had to find eventually. It wasn't how he'd expected to move on but then how does anyone do that? Maybe being dragged out of bed in the middle of the night to go on a cruise was the only way to do it.

Chapter 8

Jack Mitchell waited with his son Josh for his wife Katie to catch up with them, having strolled down Starlight's gangplank into the early morning heat. There wasn't a cloud in the sky and it was shaping up to be another great day ashore, this time in Gibraltar, a slice of Britain in the Mediterranean and a place none of them had ever been to before.

Jack had worked out they could walk straight into town from the ship, instead of using the official Galaxy shuttle buses. This would save them enough money to buy lunch somewhere, contribute to the local economy, and make him feel a bit more like a real traveller despite the convenience of having been dropped on the doorstep by a luxury cruise liner.

Josh was excited at the completely new world of cruising. Still young enough at the age of nine to find most things exciting, before the teenage attitude kicked in and made everything miserable. He and his Dad were inseparable, but it was still difficult for Jack to convince Josh that the walk into town wasn't too far or too boring, past the mostly residential and commercial buildings.

Josh was desperate to see the famous apes on the top of the rock, and Jack had promised him his first ever ride in a cable car to the summit.

After ten minutes or so they found Grand Casemates Square and followed their map down Main Street towards the cable car station, but Katie was neither a fan of heights nor animals, so suggested that they go up without her while she went back into Main Street to do some shopping.

Chapter 9

Just before midday, an unmarked police car pulled into the drop-off zone outside the port's terminal building, next to an ambulance that was just loading a stretcher in through its rear doors, watched by what must have been an officer from the ship in an all-white uniform and cap. The Spanish police officer got out of the driver's seat and popped the boot lid to remove the suitcase packed the day before. Barker still had no idea what was in it but trusted Rob not to have made a complete fool of him. He climbed out of the other side of the air-conditioned car, straightened his legs and felt the heat of the morning sun on his face before reaching into the back seat to retrieve his bag. He thanked the officer and wheeled his case into the building to show his passport and booking details to the security staff.

Regular passengers at the beginning of their cruise get their luggage taken from them and delivered to their staterooms, but John Barker was the only person boarding today. So after having his bags and himself scanned and checked, he carried them along the gangway and into Deck Four of Galaxy Starlight, the biggest ship he'd ever seen. Ten or more decks towered above him as he walked up the gangway through the opening in the starboard side of the ship, out of the cool blue daylight and into the warm artificial light of the ship's luxuriously trimmed interior.

"Mr Barker? Please, let me help you with your bags and show you to your room," said a smiling young man in a smart uniform. Barker handed his suitcase over and turned right towards the front of the ship, following the man obediently to the nearby lifts where they went up a few floors and walked out and round a corner into the longest corridor he'd ever seen, with stateroom doors on either side. The suitcase made no noise as it was wheeled along on the thick, new carpet, and about a third of the way down the young man stopped, turned to his left and stood the suitcase upright before opening the door of the room. He led Barker in and showed him around, explained the basic features and how to call for room service, before leaving him to it.

The first thing Barker noticed was the lack of a window. It was an 'inside' stateroom, probably the only type left available when Rob had booked him in, so a little small, but warm and cosy with what looked like a comfortable bed and a big TV screen on the opposite wall. Nicer than plenty of hotel rooms he'd stayed in, daylight excepted. Barker dumped his bag on the double bed on the left side of the room, picked up his mystery case and put that next to it, but decided to leave the surprise until after he'd freshened up.

Chapter 10

On a day in port, Starlight was always much quieter on board than when she was out at sea. Most of the passengers had taken the opportunity to walk off and explore the town, particularly in Gibraltar which has always been a favourite with the predominantly British passengers.

On the Lido Deck there was a hardcore of seasoned cruisers who had visited here before more than once and didn't need to get off and see it again. So they enjoyed the space and freedom to find their favourite sun loungers around the pool, or on the decks above and at the aft of the ship, and were already soaking up the sun with a paperback, having an early cocktail with their lunch, and taking the opportunity to enjoy the peace and quiet.

Most of the crew set about cleaning Starlight's pristine interior: vacuuming the carpets, tidying chairs, wiping down tables and surfaces they couldn't normally get near with all the passengers on board. The engineering team were able to carry out maintenance and repairs, and there had already been a 'man overboard' drill at 10 am involving the lowering of lifeboats and the 'rescuing' of a plastic dummy thrown into the harbour, accompanied by announcements on the ship's PA system.

The quayside was busy with passengers trickling to and fro like ants coming and going into town, coaches picking people up to go on official excursions, and forklift trucks loading and unloading food and waste from doors in Starlight's side. One of those doors was the gangway, where a lucky few crew members with half a day off walked out onto the quayside and headed for the terminal building or cafe, looking for the best Wi-Fi signal to use to send messages back home. Starlight had its own internet access, but limited bandwidth meant it was for paying passengers only.

Chapter 11

After a quick shower and shave in the tiny but functional bathroom, Barker put on the soft white robe he found hanging on the back of the bathroom door, lay down on his bed and fell asleep for an hour, tired from being woken in the early hours and being driven through the Spanish night. When he woke up he flicked on the TV and looked for a news channel to listen to while he unpacked his bags and hung his clothes up in the wardrobe by the door and familiarised himself with his room. A card on his bed told him his dinner reservation was table 201 at eight o'clock in the Four Seasons dining room, the daily Stardate newsletter told him tonight's dress code was smart casual, and a small folded map gave him an idea of what he could find inside this huge floating hotel.

With some trepidation Barker unzipped the plain black fabric suitcase. "Cheapskate," he said out loud, remembering Rob's thriftiness, but he'd done a decent job of choosing him some clothes. He'd played safe with a selection of plain formal shirts and trousers, a grey sports jacket and a cheap tuxedo for formal nights. "Me, in a tuxedo?" Barker asked himself as he glanced in the full-length mirror on the outside of the bathroom door. "Better smarten up a bit," he thought as he sucked in his stomach. He was average height for a mid-forties male, brown hair, greying at the temples, a pound or two overweight if he was honest but just tall enough to get away with it. Since he'd been alone his standards had slipped a bit and he'd lost his best feature, his smile, but at least he wouldn't stand out, for better or worse. There was standard underwear, socks, shorts for the pool, a couple of ties and two pairs of shoes, one black, one brown. Barker had thrown toiletries and medicines into a small sports bag himself, along with prescription sunglasses, a camera and a baseball cap.

He spent half an hour putting everything in its place and trying not to think too hard about the fact that this was the first room he'd unpacked in without his wife claiming her side of the bed and wardrobe and the dressing table, and looking for the hairdryer. Rather than dwell too long he noticed the lack of a kettle in the room, picked up the map of the ship's decks, and headed out to find a coffee.

Chapter 12

A perfect father-and-son day Jack thought as he and Josh sat in the cable car descending from the top of the rock of Gibraltar, approaching the final cable car station. They'd seen dozens of apes misbehaving as expected, but kept out of harm's way as Katie had instructed, and caught plenty of video footage of it on Josh's phone. The view from the top was incredible, and Josh had particularly liked the stalactites and stalagmites in the huge cave nearby.

They'd been so busy they'd eaten very little and Jack promised they would find something as soon as they got off the car. Once on Main Street again there were plenty of small restaurants to choose from but all Josh wanted was a burger, so they sat down outside the first decent place they came to and waited to order. Jack texted Katie and let her know where they were. They had half-eaten their burgers and fries by the time she appeared and sat down with them, having spent the day browsing the numerous jewellery shops and buying a bracelet Jack had said he would get for her birthday the previous week. She ordered a glass of white wine and sat while they finished their meal.

It was a fair walk back down Main Street for Josh, who had done well to keep up his enthusiasm all day, but fuelled by the burger and the promise of an ice cream in Grand Casemates Square before the final stretch back to the ship, he kept himself going.

They sat in the square for fifteen minutes watching the tourists pass by both ways, wandering in and out of the stalls and shops and bars. Then they got up and headed out through the walls towards the main road back to the port about half a mile away.

The only obstacle they had to clear was a small but busy roundabout outside the square, which they did via a couple of pedestrian crossings, watching for the green man carefully each time, and ending up walking along a single carriageway road heading straight back to the port. Halfway down the road they passed a forecourt between two apartment blocks where lots of cars were parked, paintwork bleaching in the intense heat. One or two cars passed by on the road and an engine started up somewhere near one of the apartment blocks, revving loudly as if in a hurry.

Josh had wandered ahead a few yards, allowed a little freedom on the quiet road as long as he didn't try to cross it. Katie and Jack were walking together until a scooter appeared from the apartment block doorway and drove erratically at them along the pavement, separating them by a few feet and speeding away.

Jack spun round to shout after the rider but was drowned out by the scream of an engine and the squeal of tyres, not from the scooter, but a small-engined Renault hatchback that had just started up. The car drove straight at Jack, towards the main road but onto the pavement on the way. It hit the left side of Jack's legs at close to thirty miles an hour and threw him into the air with a sickening thump as his body cartwheeled over and bounced head-and-shoulders-first off the windscreen, cracking his neck and landing about ten feet away in the main road.

Katie crumpled to the floor with her hands over her mouth staring at where Jack lay, screaming "Noooooo!" and realising that Josh was behind her. She turned and grabbed him and bundled him into a doorway and told him to wait while she went to look after Daddy. Streaming with tears, she stumbled over to Jack's motionless body and saw the pool of blood creeping out underneath him onto the tarmac. On her knees, she leaned over and touched Jack's arm and shoulder and sobbed uncontrollably. The red Renault was still accelerating away towards the town centre.

Chapter 13

I was nervous about this one. I needed help and that's always a risk. No matter how much you pay them they'll never have the same commitment. Not when it's as personal as this. But I made it worth his while. I paid him enough to buy himself a new car to replace the shit-heap one he had to burn when he got out of sight.

I needed to know whether the job had been done properly, so after I'd run through them on the scooter I abandoned it in a yard around the corner, threw my helmet in a skip and walked back down the street to where he was lying in the road with his screaming wife. I ran over to help them like the concerned citizen. I even checked his pulse. Then I dialled the police and ambulance myself, and waited with them before walking back to the ship.

I didn't expect them to have their son with them. He didn't need to see that.

Chapter 14

Just before eight o'clock, using the small folded paper map, Barker navigated from his room near the front of the ship on the starboard side, toward the Four Seasons restaurant which he could see spanned the rear, or aft, of Deck Five. Roughly halfway down the long corridor with staterooms either side, an exit on his right opened out into a lobby area where there were two large staircases on his right and four elevators on his left. He absent-mindedly pressed a button and waited.

When the lift arrived and the doors opened he was jolted back into the real world by the gaggle of people already squeezed inside the compact mirrored walls. He stepped in and turned around and tried to pretend they weren't there, forgetting to press the button for the floor he wanted until someone asked.

"Deck Five please," he replied.

"Same as everybody else then," the person said, "going for dinner?"

"Yes," Barker smiled and said nothing more.

When the doors opened he stepped into more noise as the elevator lobby opened out into the lower floor of the Atrium. A band was playing, watched by dozens of couples seated around the edge of the dance floor. Hundreds of others were flowing around the outside of the Atrium's circular perimeter, making their way past shops and cafes and wine bars on their way to or from their evening meal. Barker was a bit out of his depth, particularly on his own, but decided to just do the thing he was good at and watch what was going on and what people were up to. He was supposed to be working after all.

Table 201 was halfway down the main walkway into the Four Seasons restaurant on the port side, with a good view out to sea through a wall of windows, although the sun was on its way down and the windows were heavily tinted, making for a more subdued atmosphere inside. Arriving deliberately a few minutes late so as not to be sat on his own, Barker introduced himself to the six other guests sat at the round, eight-place table, and picked one of the empty seats between a middle-aged English woman travelling with her friend, and a couple from Australia heading home having done a grand tour of Asia and Europe. Talking to strangers had never been a problem for Barker when he was questioning them for leads in a police enquiry, but throw him into a room full of people dressed in their finest and ask him to socialise, and he felt like a fish out of water.

He managed to blend in, despite feeling uncomfortable being on his own, but decided he needed a cover story and told a white lie to the woman sat next to him, when she asked if he was travelling alone, that he was recently divorced. Still too painful to tell the truth to strangers maybe? Besides, they didn't need to know, did they? They were only going to be in his life for a few days, a few hours even, and then gone. Like her.

Laura would have loved this: the glamour, the style, the dressing up. But they had never given cruises a second thought. It was for old people, wasn't it? It wasn't like they'd had kids to

41

worry about either. They both had careers and hadn't wanted them, and then when she did get pregnant...he didn't want to think about that right now. Now he was completely alone. Even in this crowded room.

V

DAY SIX: AT SEA

Chapter 15

David Collins was an early riser. Twenty years of working shifts had meant he could never sleep past six am, even on holiday. Now he'd retired he'd had to find things to do in the mornings before his wife woke up and joined him for breakfast. He wasn't good at sitting still or pottering about in the house being quiet, so he'd taken to riding his bike or walking the dog first thing. It helped keep him fit now he wasn't working at the docks every day.

He'd never been particularly slim though. He liked his food and drink too much - work hard, play hard and all that. But he knew it was only going to get harder to keep the weight off as he got older and his activity levels decreased and his metabolism slowed down. So whenever they went on holiday he would go out for a swim or use the gym or fitness centre for an hour or so while his wife was still sleeping.

This morning he woke before six, crept out of bed and put on the shorts and T-shirt he'd left out ready, slipped on his trainers, picked up a towel and closed the stateroom door behind him as he headed out to the Fitness Centre on board Starlight.

His stateroom was near the rear of the ship so he went straight up the aft elevator and into the buffet restaurant, to grab an orange juice to wake himself up, before walking past the empty outdoor pool and up one deck. The Fitness Centre was at the front of the ship overlooking the bow cutting through the ocean towards the distant horizon. The machines were arranged all along the curved windows which extended in an arc from port to starboard, giving their users a choice of view while they burned off the excesses of the previous night.

David had tried most of the machines and didn't mind the latest technology but was a fan of the simple treadmills, particularly this early in the day, so soon after waking up. There were only one or two other people in the gym this early in the morning, so he had the place almost to himself. One man was lifting weights on the quad machine in the corner where all the serious bodybuilders would be later on. A young woman was striding out on a cross-trainer on the other side of the room, wiping her face with a small towel draped around her neck. David went to the end of the row of treadmills on the starboard side, in the corner by the door to the changing rooms. It was a quiet spot even when the place was busy, and he felt comfortable using the same machine each time, even though there were four others like it, all unoccupied.

He always started with a gentle stroll for a few minutes. He'd wasn't a natural athlete and never thought he'd enjoy running, but once he got used to warming up properly he would jog away for half an hour, sometimes with music plugged into his ears, sometimes watching a screen or – on a cruise – just admiring the view out of the window as he did this morning. Building up to a slow trot for a minute or two, he put his hands on the metal pads on the bars in front of him and monitored his heartbeat on the display panel. Sweat was working its way out and rolling down his forehead but he was settling into a good comfortable rhythm and ready to increase the pace a little to where he could keep it for a while.

David's face was glowing a healthy pink as he pressed the buttons on the screen and grabbed the handles at the side again to see if his heart rate was steady. But something didn't feel right. His right-hand tingled, then his left. His head told him to let go but somehow his hands weren't listening, if anything they were gripping tighter. Pain in the palms of his hands started to creep into his forearms and the muscles in his shoulders and across his chest tightened and he started gasping for air. His lungs weren't cooperating and he began to panic. His legs were still moving but wobbling. With what little concentration he had left he kept trying to move a hand to switch the machine off instead of just letting himself fall and maybe hurting himself. But this was hurting. The pain was becoming unbearable, the confusion incredible. Why couldn't he move his hands?

His heart stopped about five seconds later. His one hundred and eighty-pound body thumped downwards onto the moving belt and rolled off into the walkway behind, ripping his burning hands from their grip on the machine's rails. The woman on the cross trainer swung her arms and legs in time to the music on her phone and stared out of the window on the port side. The weightlifter on the machine around the corner thought he heard something as he let twenty kilos of weights down by relaxing his leg muscles. He could just see some of the treadmills but no one was on them. He saw the woman in the mirror still moving and carried on with his next set.

Chapter 16

I watched him in the gym. The same machines every time, twice a day. Creature of habit. No idea what hit him. He couldn't have made it easier for me though, repeatedly picking the treadmill nearest the wall. Nearest the sockets.

An overweight middle-aged man dies of a heart attack on a treadmill in the gym. Could there be a more textbook case? It's the most common cause of death on cruise ships, but I've used it twice now. Am I getting predictable?

Chapter 17

After a better night's sleep than he'd expected in the silence of his stateroom, Barker woke early but dozed off again until late morning. He took a quick shower and headed up to the Lido Deck to find some breakfast. In the daytime Deck Sixteen was always the busiest on Starlight. It contained the main outdoor pool in the centre of the ship and space for hundreds of sun loungers arranged around it, mostly facing in the direction of the huge screen that showed films and sports all through the day and evening. There was another deck above the Lido Deck, but around the pool area it was open and filled around the perimeter with more sun loungers.

Aft of the pool was the biggest buffet restaurant Barker had ever seen. Called Skyscape, it was accessed either port or starboard through sliding glass doors. Being quite late, it was busy with people having a late breakfast or early lunch and Barker couldn't quite believe the amount and variety of food on offer, from cereals to cold meats to hot food. Eventually, he worked out where to find what he wanted and sat down in a corner near the rear doors right at the back of the ship and ate his full English with a lukewarm coffee brought over by one of the waiters.

Suitably fed and watered, Barker found himself a sun-lounger one row back from the main pool, on a corner nearest the bar with a walkway behind him. The temperature was in the low thirties Celsius and there were just a few wispy clouds floating across the perfect blue sky. He thought maybe he'd made the right decision accepting this assignment.

Not sure of his way around the cocktail menu, he ordered a bottle of beer and sat down with his ebook reader, in just his swim shorts, bravely taking his T-shirt off revealing his pale, white, slightly overweight torso. It wasn't easy to relax, with the background music and the general din of a couple of hundred holidaymakers chatting on loungers and in whirlpools, splashing in the main pool and wandering to the bar and the twenty-four-hour Skyscape restaurant next door. The smell of burgers and pizza wafted over him from the nearby grills with their ever-present queues, fighting with the almost constant whiff of sunblock being reapplied.

He was pleasantly surprised at the mix of age groups on board. The bulk of the passengers were middle-aged, but some had their families with them and there were younger couples in their thirties and even some twentysomethings. It meant he felt he didn't stick out too much and could generally go unnoticed, apart from the empty lounger next to him on the other side of a small plastic table where his beer bottle was stood and where his wife might otherwise have been. There must be a few other single people on the ship he thought. In fact, he'd noticed special get-togethers arranged for them in Stardate, the ship's newsletter, delivered to the room every evening. Not his cup of tea.

Beer was more his thing right now, and although he was technically on duty, he didn't think another one or two would affect him too much. This was his first full day on the ship and there was plenty of time for work. He picked up his bottle and swallowed the last half an inch of lager inside it and swung his legs off to the left side of the sun lounger so he could stand up out of the way of passers-by. He put down his Kindle and hid it under a spare towel and headed towards the bar on his right.

As he did so a woman in a bright yellow one-piece swimsuit climbed slowly up the steps out of the corner of the pool on his left-hand side in a perfect Bond-movie moment. Her coffee-coloured skin matched her choice of swimwear in a confident way that only someone with a perfect figure could pull off. She was about five-foot-ten with long black hair stuck to her head and neck by the water running off her head and down her shoulders, chest and arms. Keep moving, he thought, don't stare. So he turned his head back in the direction he was heading and immediately came to a crashing halt, bouncing off a young woman in a small, blue-and-white floral bikini, emptying the drink in her left-hand and knocking the paperback in her right to the floor.

It would have been awkward if they'd both been fully clothed, but half-naked as they both were, the full torso-to-torso contact added a layer of weirdness to an already embarrassing moment.

"Oh God I'm sorry!" Barker said in a fluster, stepping back and noticing the remains of the woman's Mojito trickling down her left shoulder, across her breast and into her cleavage, before realising he was staring again.

"Don't worry," said the woman, looking down at the spilt drink and wet paperback book on the deck, "I've got a free drinks package!"

She looked up and to Barker's relief had a smile on her face, "I'd be upset if I was wearing a dress."

"I'm really sorry, I don't know what happened. Can I get you another drink?" Barker said.

"No, it doesn't matter really."

"No it does, hang on," said Barker as he strode the couple of remaining steps to the bar, where he deposited his empty beer bottle, ordered a Mojito and picked up a handful of paper napkins to hand to the woman to dry herself.

"Thanks," she said, "But I'll just go and have a shower by the pool. I was going for a swim anyway."

"OK," Barker said, "That was so embarrassing, I'm sorry. It's my first cruise and I'm still finding my way around."

The barman returned with her cocktail and Barker passed it on with an apologetic smile.

"Thank you," the woman said as she turned and walked away alongside the bar, turning left behind the opposite side of the pool and disappearing behind a group of people climbing out of a hot tub.

Barker breathed in and out slowly, ordered himself another beer and went and sat down on his lounger. He applied more sun cream and decided to stay put rather than risk getting into any more trouble.

"Is this one free?" said a voice on his left-hand side.

Barker looked up and saw the girl in the blue-and-white bikini standing over him, dripping wet, and pointing at the empty lounger next to his.

"Er...yes. Yes, if you think it's safe to sit next to me," he replied.

She smiled, and asked, "Your wife won't mind?"

The word 'wife' hit Barker like a bullet, entering his head and making it spin, catching his throat as it headed down and making him feel sick in the stomach as it made its way out.

"No," he said curtly, the smile draining from his face. "I'm on my own."

The woman had two towels over her shoulder, one of which she lay down on the lounger to sit on, and the other she proceeded to dry herself down with. She was an attractive woman. Average height and build, slightly curvy, with a bob of short black hair. Her face was round with full lips and sparkly blue eyes, and she was probably at least ten years younger than him.

Not that he'd noticed.

Barker tried to distract himself by swigging from his bottle and pretending to read his Kindle for a few moments until the woman sat sideways on her lounger facing his and said, "I'm Lucy, Lucy Jones," and held out her hand.

"John Barker," he replied.

"Nice to meet you John Barker," said Lucy, "Your first cruise then?"

"Yes, it's all a bit new and weird at the minute. Not quite sure how everything works, still finding my feet."

"And what do you think of it all?"

"Impressive. Beautiful ship, food's great. I'm just not used to this sort of luxury."

"Can I be cheeky and pinch some of that?" said Lucy, pointing at the bottle of sun lotion on the table between their loungers, "I've left mine in my stateroom."

"What? Oh yes, of course. Help yourself," said Barker, aware that this meant she was about to apply his sun lotion over her body, and he would have to at least look in her direction while she did it if she continued to talk to him.

"You need to find a woman," Rob had said. *Not this bloody quickly*, he thought to himself.

He'd been completely happily married for twenty years and being in the company of women whilst being newly single - widowed - was a completely alien feeling to him. Of course he'd mixed with women in his police career, but as a married man, and most of his female colleagues were married. And they all been in a stressful job, and not chilled, happy and wearing a bikini by a pool on a cruise ship. Different kettle of fish.

"So what about you? Have you done this before? You don't look like a regular cruiser," said Barker.

"Ha! No, I work here," Lucy replied. "Not crew of course. I wouldn't be here if I was. I'm entertainment staff, so I sometimes sneak out on deck when I get time off. I'm a singer."

"Oh wow," said Barker, impressed, "That must keep you busy."

"Yeah, very. Three or four slots a day, every day. Hence why I sneak out here whenever I can to catch some sun and fresh air."

"What sort of stuff do you sing?"

"Bit of everything. Soul, blues, pop. You should come and watch sometime."

"You'll think I'm stalking you."

"No! It would be no good if nobody came to watch me would it?" Lucy swivelled around and straightened her legs out on the lounger and lay back, closing her eyes and soaking up the sun's warmth. "I'm in the Atrium every afternoon if you're passing."

Chapter 18

An elderly man shuffled out of a doorway into a corridor inside St. Bernard's hospital in Gibraltar. His face was ashen. He was supported on his left-hand side by a younger woman, his daughter Helen, tears running down her cheeks.

"I need to go home," the man said.

"OK Dad, but we'll have to find a hotel for tonight, it's late," his daughter replied.

"No, I want to go home."

"Dad, we have to arrange for the body..." she stopped herself, "For Mum to be transported home. We can't do that now, everyone's going home. We'll have to come back in the morning and do it then."

"Can't I go now?"

"You need to rest Dad."

A woman wearing a uniform emerged from the same doorway behind them and shouted after them.

"Mr Gibson? Mr Gibson?"

They both stopped and began to turn towards the woman as she caught up with them.

"I rang the Bristol hotel, not too far away. They have rooms available tonight. Ask reception to arrange a taxi for you, they'll know where it is."

"That's very kind, thank you," said Helen.

"Not at all. I'm not here in the morning but my colleague Louise will look after you."

Edward and Helen turned and linked arms again and walked down the long, empty corridor.

"I wasn't ready for her to go Helen."

"No Dad, neither was I."

"I know we're not spring chickens, but she was so bright and healthy. I would never have let her go on her own if I'd thought she was sick."

"She wasn't sick Dad, it was her heart. None of us know if that's going to happen."

"I just wish I'd been with her when it happened. I'll never forgive myself for that."

"You can't think that Dad. She was enjoying herself. She loved cruises, and you knew that and let her go even though you couldn't be with her. That was the right thing to do."

"And now we have to take her home in a box."

"I'll sort it all tomorrow Dad. You can stay in the hotel if you want. I'll come back and sort it all out."

As they emerged from the large service lift into the reception foyer and approached the reception desk, a middle-aged man in a crumpled suit stumbled through the entrance door and up to the desk. Breathlessly he paused to ask the young woman behind the desk a question and turned to head towards the lift, narrowly avoiding Edward and Helen coming the other way before stopping and turning around.

"Edward? Edward Gibson?" he said.

"Stephen?" replied Edward.

"Edward, what on earth are you doing in Gibraltar?"

"It's my wife Stephen. She..."

"She passed away," interrupted Helen.

"Oh God no," Stephen said, staring at them in confusion. "Edward...My son. My son died this afternoon in a road accident."

All three looked at one another in stunned silence.

"Stephen, I'm going to take my father to the Bristol hotel for the night and put him to bed," Helen began. "If you need somewhere to stay they have rooms available. You can meet me there later if you like. You have Dad's number? I'll keep his phone with me."

"Yes...Yes, thanks Helen. I'll do that. Excuse me, I've to got to...I've got to go."

Stephen turned and ran towards the lift.

Chapter 19

Lucy stayed on the Lido Deck for about twenty minutes before heading back to work when Barker appeared to have nodded off. He woke shortly after and sipped his beer and read his book for another hour or so. He didn't see the woman in the yellow swimsuit again, but she'd reminded him of the photos on his phone and that he was really here for work, not pleasure. He justified a little rest after travelling through the night to get to the ship, but in his first twenty-four hours on board he had seen little more than the inside of his windowless stateroom, the restaurants and the Lido Deck. There were plenty more parts of the ship to see, and places where he might meet people.

Back in his stateroom, Barker looked at the images he'd downloaded onto his phone the night before last. They were a bit fuzzy, but it was perfectly possible that the woman he'd seen climbing out of the pool was the woman in these images. Rob was right, she did stand out from the crowd, but what were the chances of spotting her so soon. Her hair was pinned up in the first photo, and he could only see her head and shoulders from her right side. But the skin tone was similar and hair colour a little lighter. The second was almost face-on, the long dark hair very similar. But he hadn't looked at her for long enough, before bumping into Lucy, to be sure it was her.

Barker looked around for the map of the ship he'd been given the day before, but couldn't find it, so he decided to head out again and use the diagrams of the ship that were fixed to the walls by every staircase and elevator, and the entrance to every major room, showing what deck you were on, where you were, and all the main places of interest. He could have used the app that paired with his Sea Star and located him anywhere on the ship but, being a bit old-school, he felt he'd remember the layout better if he learned it the old way. Above Deck Nine where his room was, there were only hundreds more staterooms, spread over six or seven more floors until you reached the Lido Deck where he'd just come from, so he decided to go down to Deck Eight and the top of the Atrium and work his way down from there.

There were bars everywhere: wine bar, gin bar, cocktail bar, piano bar, as well as a speciality coffee shop, a Deli, a casino with dozens of machines and tables where the guests could spend their cash, and even an art gallery with original paintings that would be auctioned at various points during the cruise. The Emporium on Deck Five consisted of half a dozen spotless boutiques full of designer watches, clothes, handbags and jewellery at eye-watering prices. Not far away was the Spa, offering beauty treatments at prices that Barker thought he'd need a massage to recover from.

After an hour or more inside the lower decks Barker got in a lift and went as high as it would go: Deck Eighteen. Pushing a door open to the outer deck he wandered around basketball courts, putting greens, more pools and sun-loungers, and back inside found more bars, a photo studio and the largest gym he'd ever seen, full of treadmills, exercise bikes and rowing machines, and dozens of sweaty holidaymakers trying to make sure their clothes would still fit during the second week of the cruise.

Eventually, satisfied he had covered pretty much everywhere he was allowed to go, and a little overloaded with new information, Barker didn't think he could do anymore and decided to sample one of those bars.

Chapter 20

Helen Gibson walked unsteadily into the residents' lounge of the Bristol Hotel and found a seat in a quiet corner by a window, looking out onto the darkening town streets. A text had come through from Stephen Mitchell when Helen was alone in her room, sobbing, after sending her father to bed. Stephen said he would be staying in the hotel and asked if she would meet him in the bar. She could have done with some sleep but thought a couple of drinks might help her relax.

The bar was virtually empty, except for a couple of residents sat together on the other side of the room. She could hear voices beyond them in reception, a guest checking in. Soon after, Stephen walked in through the door, looking every inch like a man who'd just had the worst news ever. Helen stood and straightened her clothes as best she could for a woman who'd just lost her mother.

Stephen's eyes were as red as hers, from the tears they'd both shed in the last twenty-four hours. Helen was uncertain how to greet him, but he wrapped his arms around her and squeezed without saying a word. For most it would have been an uncomfortably long hug, if understandable in the circumstances. For them it was the first time they'd touched since their affair that had ended Stephen's marriage to the mother of his son, the son whose body he'd just identified.

"Stephen I'm so sorry," whispered Helen, "What happened?"

"Hit and run. Not far from the port," Stephen replied, looking at the floor.

"Oh no, that's awful."

"Katie and Josh were with him. They saw it Helen, they saw him die. A few minutes earlier and they'd have been back on the ship."

"Ship? Which ship? Not the Starlight?" Helen asked.

"Yes, Galaxy Starlight. Why?"

"That's the one Mum was on when... when she died." Helen stumbled over the words.

"Jesus Helen, what's going on?"

"It was a stroke or a heart attack, we're not a hundred percent sure yet. Jack was on the same ship?"

"Yes, from Southampton, heading for the Caribbean."

A waiter approached and asked what they'd like to drink. Stephen ordered a whiskey and Helen a gin and tonic. As the waiter walked away they looked at each other, through the windows, at the floor, both stunned and searching for the next thing to say.

"Oh Helen, your Dad must be in a state," Stephen said.

"Yes, he's not good. He's been going downhill since he left the business...I'm worried this could finish him off."

"Was he with Margaret when...?"

"No he wasn't on the cruise. He had some meeting to go to. Something to do with the handover. He told Mum to go by herself. He knew...he thought she'd be safe. What about Jack's Mum?"

"Linda? She's on her way. I was driving on the M25 when I

got the call, so I just jumped on the first flight out of Heathrow. She'll arrive in the early hours some time. I've booked her a room."

"Awkward."

"I know. I'm sorry. I wasn't thinking straight."

"It's OK. It doesn't matter in the circumstances. I'll be out early to the hospital. I just want to get it over with."

Starlight headed southwest overnight, leaving the relative calm of the Mediterranean Sea and sailing out into the Atlantic Ocean, bound for Fort Lauderdale where she would be based for her winter season in the Caribbean. There would be another stop after a day and two nights at sea at Funchal on the Island of Madeira, and another, some days later at Nassau, the Bahamian capital, before heading for Florida.

VI

DAY SEVEN: MADEIRA

Chapter 21

A little over five hundred miles and nineteen hours from Gibraltar, the Portuguese island of Madeira was bathed in sunshine as Starlight approached the harbour in Funchal just before 11 am the next morning.

Feeling restless, Barker had been up since seven, wandering as casually as he could through the busy Skyscape restaurant keeping his eyes open for his mystery woman, just in case she was sat having breakfast. Rob had not given her a name in his email, simply saying that she was wanted on both sides of the Atlantic, but hadn't been seen for two years and was presumed dead.

In his own head Barker had simply nicknamed her 'Yellow' because of the swimming costume she was wearing when he first saw her. If she wanted to be off the ship for an official excursion she would have to eat early. But maybe not this early. He sat down and ate breakfast twice. Cereal and juice in the restaurant on the port side of the ship, and half an hour later bacon and eggs on the starboard side. This sort of thing wasn't his speciality. He was more used to tracking stolen goods and drug shipments than finding missing persons.

After giving up in the restaurant he wandered through the inside of the ship, looking in the empty bars and shops, eventually finding himself up on the top deck watching the ship manoeuvre into the harbour. He was fascinated by how accurately and delicately such a large machine could be nudged into position. And he could also check out the other passengers who were doing the same thing. No sign of her.

Obviously, she was still on board right now, so he just had to watch if she went ashore, where she went, and that she eventually got back on board, although he couldn't think of a reason why anyone, even a fugitive, would want to jump ship on a small mid-Atlantic island.

But he was out of practice. He'd given up being a police officer and his brain wasn't tuned-in any more. He needed to at least go through the motions to get himself back into the groove of an investigation. If that's what this was.

He made his way down to Deck Four to wait somewhere near the staircase where all the passengers going ashore would have to file past him. If anyone asked he could pretend to be 'waiting for his wife'.

The flow of people began to grow and Barker stood out of the way, to one side of the central bank of elevators opposite the main staircase, watching as best he could the mostly middle-aged throng shuffle down the stairs and hoped there were no other routes out to the gangway that he was missing. After what felt like an hour but was more like fifteen minutes, he caught a glimpse of the head of a woman in the group leaving the lift furthest away from him and making their way towards the staircase. She was taller than most of the others, with long, straight, almost-black hair and olive skin. He remembered he'd only ever seen this woman once before, and that was in a soaking wet swimsuit, climbing out of a pool.

Barker decided he had no choice but to assume she was the

woman he'd seen and joined the back of the group and followed them down the stairs, fishing his Sea Star wristband out of his pocket so the staff could scan him off the ship. As they were doing so he tried to keep his eye on his target, who was four places in front and stepping quickly down the gangway. He had a sudden thought that if she was booked onto one of Galaxy's very expensive guided tours, she would probably walk straight onto one of the coaches in the facing car park and he wouldn't be able to follow her. He hadn't thought this through very well.

As he stepped out into the bright daylight and down from the gangway he looked straight ahead to the waiting coaches but had lost sight of her. To his right was the cruise terminal offices, the stern of the ship and the end of the jetty. To his left was a road leading out of the port complex, with a pavement on the left-hand side, filled with a snake of ambling tourists heading into town, one or two looking for taxis, others holding out paper maps looking for landmarks. Near the back of the snake was the tall, dark-haired woman he'd watched leave the lift. He turned and followed.

Barker worried how he was going to stay behind her without catching her up or looking conspicuous, but pretty soon found the problem was keeping up with her. Dressed in flat shoes, tight blue jeans (in this heat) and a red vest top, Yellow looked almost like a local going to work rather than a tourist just off a luxury cruise ship, as she strode purposefully past the young and elderly alike, hopping off and on the pavement to make her way through the crowd.

Just outside the harbour entrance a modern, red double-decker bus with an open roof was parked at the side of the road with its engine running, waiting eagerly for passengers.

Barker bought a ticket as he followed the woman onto the bus, but stayed downstairs when she went up. He put the headphones hanging by his seat over his ears like everybody else immediately did, and fumbled for the language selection and volume controls so he could hear the commentary. He had no idea where they were going or what he was going to do if Yellow came down and got off the bus on her own.

Barker spotted a route plan on the upper wall of the bus on the other side of the aisle. It seemed to show that the return leg of the circular journey would be more scenic and that the journey into the town this way would not take long. Third stop probably. But just before the second one he heard footsteps coming down the stairs. Female footsteps.

Sure enough, Yellow stepped out of the staircase into the aisle by the driver, glancing briefly down the back of the bus before turning and holding the rail near the door as the bus began to slow down. Barker's heart started pumping hard. He had to decide what to do. They were only on the edge of the town centre, so he couldn't just get off and amble aimlessly like any other tourist. He had to have a purpose, or at least look like he did. The bus came to a final stop and the doors hissed open. Yellow stepped confidently off and before Barker could make his mind up, four other people behind him stood up and shuffled past him towards the door at the front of the bus.

Trying to make it look like it had been his plan all along, he joined them, smiled at the bus driver, and stepped off onto the pavement, looking around as if to get his bearings, but really just wondering where the woman had gone.

Not far, as it turned out. Fifty yards away on the corner of a street was a small coffee shop with tables and chairs outside, next to a couple of touristy gift shops. He just caught sight of Yellow as she walked through the café door, and headed that way, skipping past the other four tourists who'd got off the bus and were working out what to do next.

Barker knew he couldn't just walk straight in behind the woman, so mooched around outside the gift shop next door for a couple of minutes. By the time he'd decided it was reasonable to wander into the café, she was on her way back out again. In fact she smiled at Barker and held the door open for him to go inside. Flustered, Barker blushed like a schoolboy, said, 'Thank you,' and looked back a little too obviously as he walked inside. Yellow sat herself down at one of the tables outside the door.

"Ola Señor, what can I get for you?" said the apron-wearing man behind the counter, "Coffee?"

"Yes, please...Latte. Decaf." Barker replied.

"Take a seat sir, and I'll bring it right over."

"Thanks."

There were a handful of other customers inside but plenty of room for him to choose a quiet spot on his own where he could look out through the glass front of the café. He perched on a stool at a narrow table against a wall next to a rack of brochures aimed at tourists, mainly so he could have something to do while he sat waiting for and, hopefully, drinking his coffee.

A waiter walked past with a small tray and pushed open the door, turning to his left and placing the tray on the table where Yellow was sat admiring the view back towards the port with her sunglasses on, playing with her iPhone. Seconds later the man he had spoken to appeared beside him with another tray with a large milky latte in a glass with a tiny handle, placed on a small saucer with what looked like a small wrapped chocolate

71

on it.

Conscious that he might have to leave at short notice, Barker read the drinks menu on the table and found a five-Euro note in his pocket and placed it on the table under the saucer. He picked out a leaflet at random, opened it up and pretended to read it while keeping half an eye out of the front window.

It seemed Yellow was going to enjoy her coffee. From what he could tell she wasn't texting anyone and certainly not making any calls, just idly swiping at the screen as if browsing through photos, maybe just passing the time. But why?

Almost five minutes had passed and Barker's latte had cooled to a drinkable temperature, when another red open-top bus pulled into a stop on the opposite side of the road from where they'd got off, probably on its way back towards the port. Yellow calmly stood up, swung her handbag over her shoulder, slipped her phone inside the bag and made a beeline across the road and around the back of the bus.

Barker's heart pounded again as he faced another decision. How could he follow her now? One person jumping straight back on the bus was unusual, two was suspicious, and having bumped into her in the doorway and *then* following her would make it stalking. Which, of course he was.

So he resigned himself to not following and admitted defeat. He just wasn't good at this. He would look for her again on the ship tomorrow. And he remembered hearing an announcement before they left Gibraltar for a Mr & Mrs Mitchell, who had presumably not got back on board in time, so he would no doubt hear an announcement for this woman, whatever her name was, if she failed to show up. Barker watched the bus leave, finished his coffee, paid and walked outside.

He thought about heading left and into the town to explore. He'd never been to Madeira before and he needed to settle nerves a bit, so he wandered to the bus stop where he'd got off earlier and waited, hoping there'd be another one along in a minute.

From where he stood Barker could see across the road to the stop heading back to the port where Yellow had jumped back on the bus. On the road was a small, bright piece of metal glinting in the sun. He remembered his own wristband, looked down at it, and looked up again. He stepped out and crossed the road to the other bus stop and picked up the metal disc – another Sea Star from Galaxy Starlight, with the star sign Aires etched on it over a light blue background, the sign of a first-timer on Galaxy cruises. Around the edge of the disc was printed the name Maria Cortez.

Chapter 22

Within an hour Barker was back on the ship and in his state-room looking for his cell phone. He dialled Rob's number. It would be mid-afternoon back home so he should be at work. Rob answered surprisingly quickly.

"Hey John! How's it going? Topped up the tan?" Rob shouted.

"Hi Rob, no not much. But I've found your woman." Barker replied.

"Really? So soon? Nice one. Are you sure it's her?"

"I'm sure she's the woman in the photos you sent me. Are you going to tell me her name?"

"Not allowed to give you any info John – need-to-know and all that."

"Does the name Maria Cortez mean anything to you?" Barker asked.

"Not particularly John, but she is Latin-American. It could be an alias. Doesn't mean much on its own."

"Why all the secrecy?"

"You know as much as I do mate. We've just been told she's wanted and had been missing. So we want to find out where she goes."

"So it's not just a cruise? I have to follow her when we get off?" Barker asked, annoyed.

"Maybe John, just for a day or two. And then let us know what you find."

"I'm not James bloody Bond Rob,' said Barker, letting his frustration show."

"Oh I don't know John, I bought you a tuxedo didn't I?"

"So that's it? Is there anything else you're going to tell me? Maybe I'll keep my phone switched off and just get on the plane home."

"Calm down John, no need to be like that. Just keep an eye on her and let us know. But don't ring every day in case someone's listening in."

"Listening in? This is bigger than you're letting on isn't it Rob?"

"Standard procedure John. Relax. You've got almost a week to chill out on that ship now. Enjoy it."

"Bye Rob."

Barker turned his phone off, threw it on his bed and took Maria Cortez's Sea Star down to the customer services desk on Deck Five to hand it in. He couldn't think how she'd got back on the ship without it, unless she carried her passport with her as well. He was sick of worrying about it. If Rob wouldn't tell him anything why should he care? She wasn't going anywhere for now, so he decided to put her out of his mind as Rob had suggested, and get on with enjoying the ship. If he met Ms Cortez again, all well and good. If not, there were more important things in life.

Chapter 23

Starlight left the port of Funchal around four in the afternoon. Barker had spent a couple of hours on a lounger on the starboard side of the ship facing the town, watching the comings and goings of the ship's passengers and the local people and traffic going about their everyday business, oblivious to, or maybe dependent on, the cruise ship docked on the edge of their neighbourhood. He'd picked up a book from the small ship's library and read the first couple of chapters but he wasn't really in the mood for reading. He wasn't very good at relaxing. Too much time to think.

As the view of land on the horizon slipped away sideways, replaced by open water, Barker remembered Lucy Jones. 'I'm in the Atrium every afternoon,' she'd said. The thought was enough to make him sit up and swivel off the side of his lounger and stand up, thinking there could be worse ways to spend an hour. It made him think of Laura again and his stomach rolled over. He took a deep breath of sea air, straightened himself and walked in through the double doors onto the corridor of Deck Seven.

The inside of the ship was busy with people passing an hour or two before going for dinner. Music played from the small bars dotted around the decks as Barker made his way towards the Atrium in the middle of the ship, where grand staircases flowed up and down between Decks Five to Eight. At the bottom, a circular marble floor about twenty-five feet across was surrounded by upholstered chairs and small round tables. Barker arrived at the top floor and heard the sound of a woman singing. Looking over the railings he could see Lucy three decks below him, stood in front of a small house band consisting of a pianist, a drummer and a couple of guitarists. The staircases had the effect of making people feel they were making an entrance, which indeed they were. Barker felt self-conscious as he walked down the three flights and found a spare seat almost directly across from the band and sat down.

Lucy's voice was strong and soulful, better than he'd expected. Not that he was any kind of expert. He ordered a drink from a waiter that passed by and settled down to lose himself in something other than his memories or his mission to follow Ms Cortez. Lucy sang half a dozen other songs, a mix of rock, blues and country hits suited to the middle-aged crowd, but delivered with passion and flair. Barker was impressed, as was the appreciative audience, applauding generously after each song. Being on the front row he was conscious he might be seen to be staring a bit too much, so he balanced it by looking up and down the decks at the people leaning over the railings watching the band, or walking up and down the staircases. There were never these awkward moments when he was with Laura. As a couple you can talk to each other in-between times, but on your own there was no other distraction, so you had to find something to focus on. So he was taken by surprise when Lucy finished her last song, thanked the assembled crowd and walked directly across the floor towards him.

Lucy was wearing a bright red jumpsuit with a plunging neckline, matching red lipstick and a beaming smile. John's pulse raced a little as he realised she was looking in his direction. It may only be a cruise ship house band, but the star of the show was heading straight over to him.

"Hello John, may I join you?" said Lucy, sitting down at the spare chair across the small round wooden table from his.

"Of course," he smiled, hoping he didn't look like the awkward teenager he felt like inside, "That was fantastic."

"Thank you!" Lucy said, genuinely pleased with the compliment, "Can I have a G-and-T please Jose?" she asked the waiter walking past their table.

"Certainly Miss Jones," the waiter replied with a smile.

"Thanks for coming to watch," Lucy said, "I didn't know if you would. What have you been up to since I last saw you?"

"Not a lot," Barker replied, "I went off the ship for an hour or so earlier but didn't go far. Then I read for a bit...bit of people-watching, you know."

With his next breath Barker caught the smell of Lucy's perfume. She smelled as good as she looked. Behind her, half a dozen couples had started circling the floor to a waltz being played on the sound system now that the band had gone for a break.

"Did you see any more of the woman in the yellow swimsuit?" said Lucy out of nowhere.

"What? Sorry, who?" Barker replied, a little taken aback.

"You know, the woman you were staring at when you bumped into me," Lucy said, smiling at Barker's embarrassment. "It's OK, she was gorgeous. I was looking at her myself."

"Oh, no. No, I haven't."

"You should try to find her John. You never know your luck. If you're single..."

"I'm sure she's not alone. Probably got a gorgeous husband somewhere. And I never said I was single."

"So how come you're here on your own?"

Barker opened his mouth to reply, uncertain of exactly what to say, but before any words came out there was a sharp crack, a dull thud and, all in a split second, the crash of a tall, thin elderly man onto the table between himself and Lucy. There was no Hollywood collapse of furniture, just a sickening crumpling of the man's body over the round wooden surface, and the beginnings of confusion amongst the crowd as his body slipped onto the floor, brushing Lucy's shins.

The taped music continued to play in the background but the dancers had stopped, frozen. For a few seconds there was no other noise while the situation sank in, then a few quiet gasps from the people close by. Until they saw the blood.

Lucy's face had a few small red spots dotted at random across her left cheek. There were spots of dark red on her scarlet jumpsuit. Looking down, Barker saw a dark red patch just below the man's left collar bone on his pale blue shirt. It looked like a bullet wound.

Barker's first aid training kicked in and he stood up and stepped over to Lucy and leaned over the man at her feet who was twisted but roughly lying on his back. There was no response, but he felt a pulse in the man's wrist. He pulled a handkerchief out of his pocket and pressed it onto the wound.

The onlookers had started to panic and the noise level was rising with a few squeals from the lady dancers and general hubbub as they all moved away. Nearby staff had seen the commotion and a bartender ran to summon the ship's medical staff. Lucy pushed back her chair to give the man some room. Barker held the soaked cotton pad on the man's chest and looked around for something else more substantial to replace it, without success. He instinctively scanned the surrounding balconies for any sign of danger, but they were filling up with more passengers wondering what the commotion was all about.

A medic appeared with a bag and two other staff carrying a stretcher. The medic thanked Barker and asked him to move away, replacing his handkerchief with a more substantial dressing pressed onto the wound. Lucy looked at Barker and their eyes maintained contact for several seconds as if asking each other if they'd seen the same thing just happen. Lucy's face had gone white. Barker moved around to the side of her chair and squatted by it, watching the medic work, waiting to see if he could help. The men with the stretcher placed it by the man on the floor and carefully shuffled him onto it, standing up and carrying him away with the medic following. Suddenly, apart from the blood on the floor, it was all over.

Just as the remaining people standing around were gathering their senses and wondering what to do there were clunking sounds from the four corners of each of the Atrium decks, as the large doors were closed around them. Then a voice said, 'Ladies and gentlemen, please stay where you are while I take your names in case we need to ask you any questions. I know some of you will be dining soon. I won't keep you long.'

The voice belonged to Michael Brennan, head of the ship's security team, and Lucy's surprise stateroom guest from the first day of the cruise.

"He was shot Michael," said Lucy as he walked over.

"Are you OK?" Brennan asked, "You don't look too good."

"I'm fine. Well...shaken but... Michael, somebody just shot him," Lucy replied, still stunned.

"Well, we'll see what we find when we get him to the treatment room."

"I've seen a bullet wound before," interrupted Barker, standing up

Brennan looked at Barker and said, "And you are?"

"John Barker," he replied.

"Thanks for your help Mr Barker. Did you see what happened?"

"No," said Barker, shaking his head. "I heard a cracking sound and then the shattering of glass as he fell on the table."

"Well, we'll speak to everyone here eventually and get as good a picture of what happened as we can."

Brennan turned to two other uniformed security staff and instructed them to take the names and room numbers of the dancers and the people sat in or stood around the chairs next to the dance floor.

Barker noticed other security staff starting to appear on the floors above, speaking to people watching the events from the balconies. He looked at Lucy and said, "Come on, you need a drink."

"I need a shower," she said.

"Brandy first, shower later."

Chapter 24

Useless idiot! Or am I the stupid one for letting him try? If you want a job done properly...

All the trouble he went to getting into position and he doesn't finish him off. And then he gets himself caught trying to hide the gun in the kitchens.

That might be a blessing in disguise though. At least the witnesses will think it's all over. I'll be more careful next time. And I'll do it alone.

Chapter 25

"Right, that'll do," said Lucy, having swallowed a shot of brandy at the bar, "I really do need a shower. I've got blood on me, and it's not mine."

"Luckily," Barker said.

"Listen, John, don't take this the wrong way, but will you come back to my room with me and watch TV or something while I shower? I don't really want to be on my own at the minute. I'm still shaking." Lucy asked.

"If you want me to," Barker answered.

He followed Lucy out of the bar to the mid-ships staircase. They avoided the lifts and walked down a couple of decks and out through the casino and into a corridor down towards Lucy's stateroom. Inside it was pretty much the same as his but with a more fragrant smell. A few clean clothes were laid out on the bed and dirty ones on the floor.

"Oh, shit, sorry," said Lucy, running around picking them up and throwing them in the bottom of the wardrobe.

"Don't worry, mine's the same," John lied, knowing how he always put everything in its place.

A little red light was flashing on the phone by the bed. Lucy picked up the receiver and pressed the button to hear her messages.

"Entertainment's off for this evening. At least in the Atrium and on the Lido Deck," said Lucy.

"Night off?"

"Yes," said Lucy with relief in her voice, "I could do with it, to be honest. Listen, the TV remote's on the sofa, help yourself. I won't be long."

"Take your time."

Lucy went into the tiny bathroom and turned on the shower. Barker sat down and flicked the TV on. He didn't have time to settle down and watch a film so he just flicked through the channels, looking at what was available: movies, sports, news, business, the usual stuff. Plus the onboard information channels and the ship's webcam fitted to the bridge looking straight ahead. It was dark outside so the view was black.

In less than ten minutes the shower stopped and the bathroom door clicked open to let the steam out. A few seconds later Lucy stepped out wrapped in a towel that didn't quite reach down to her knees. She was just finishing drying her short black hair with a hand towel.

"Listen John, I'm sorry I took the mickey out of you before. It's just my way," she said.

"What do you mean?" Barker replied, knowing full well.

"About that woman by the pool. I was just winding you up. It's none of my business why you're here on your own and you don't need me teasing you."

"That's OK," said Barker, noting the irony of her not wanting to tease him whilst wearing a small towel.

"And I've only just noticed the ring on your finger, now that you're sat in my room with me half-dressed. I'm sorry, you can go if want. You're too polite."

"She died..." Barker blurted, stunning himself as much as

Lucy, "My wife. She took her own life," he continued, looking up at Lucy. Her mouth moved but no words came out.

"Sorry, now I'm saying things I don't need to and making you feel bad," said Barker, looking at the floor.

Lucy put her hand over her mouth and her eyes began to glisten.

"She was working late in the forensic lab. I was due to pick her up. I was late. Too late. She was beaten up by burglars and left for dead. She lost her baby. Our baby."

"Oh my God John, I'm so sorry. Did they catch anyone?" Lucy whispered.

"No. She recovered...from the bruises...but not from losing the baby. It tore her apart. She couldn't take it..."

"John, I'm so sorry."

Neither spoke for a few seconds.

"Is that where you worked?" asked Lucy.

"No. I was a policeman. That's how we met."

"Was?"

"I walked out after Laura died. Been twiddling my thumbs for the last six months."

Barker stared at the floor. Lucy sat down on the sofa next to him.

"What was she like?"

"Tall, pretty, long brown hair, nice eyes. Always calm and kind."

"I don't know what to say John. Today must've been awful for you."

"Yes and no. Never going to be as bad as that was."

He took a deep breath, stood up and straightened his shirt.

"I'd better get myself cleaned up too. Dinner's in an hour. What are you going to do?"

"No idea. I'm not used to having a free evening."

"There's a spare seat at my table. Pick you up in forty-five minutes?"

Lucy smiled and nodded, "Yeah, see you then," and closed the door behind him.

Chapter 26

When he opened his stateroom door, Barker found a note pushed under it, on headed paper. It read,

An incident occurred in the Atrium this afternoon in which a passenger was seriously injured. The ship's security team are conducting an ongoing investigation, and a suspect has been detained. We ask for calm following this incident and promise we will keep all passengers informed. Events on the ship will not be affected as we believe there is no further danger to other passengers. Thank you for your understanding.

"Hmmm," Barker muttered.

He stripped and jumped straight into the shower, dried off, shaved and picked out a clean shirt. He realised he was thinking about how others might see him for the first time in a long time, and he had scrubbed up quite well.

Twenty minutes later Barker walked back down the corridor to Lucy's room, checked his watch, and knocked on the door. Lucy opened it almost immediately. She was wearing a short, silver, sequinned dress, strappy sandals that wound up her ankles, and carrying a small silver handbag.

"Wow," Barker said involuntarily.

"Too much?" Lucy asked.

"No, no, I didn't mean that."

"Sorry, I packed for being on stage not for quiet evenings out," Lucy said as she stepped out and closed the door behind her.

"You look great. I'm not good at compliments. How are you feeling?"

"Better thanks, more chilled. How about you?"

"Like I'm on a date," Barker said nervously as they walked down the corridor.

"Ha!" Lucy laughed, "John Barker, will you take me to dinner?"

Chapter 27

Barker had the best evening of the cruise so far, possibly the best he'd had in a long time. Considering a man had been shot next to him earlier in the day and brought the memories of his wife flooding back again, he was surprised at how relaxed he felt. The restaurant had fewer people in it than usual, but was noisier. The afternoon's events were buzzing all over the place. He and Lucy were the stars of the show at their table, partly because they'd been present in the Atrium in the middle of things, partly because Lucy brought some glamour and a bit of stardust to the table, and also simply because John had arrived with a young woman, having been on his own the past two nights. It was all so exciting.

"What I don't get is why they haven't turned the ship around," said Jared, one of the American men across the table.

"Well they say they've got somebody," said Angela, from Berkshire, "Why ruin it for everyone else?"

"I hope you're right," said David, Jared's partner.

"Has this sort of thing happened before Lucy?" asked Angela.

"Not that I'm aware of," Lucy said, "There are accidents, illnesses and stuff, the odd scuffle sometimes when people drink too much. I have heard of a crew member going missing once. Don't know whether he jumped or was pushed."

"Or went in the curry!" shouted David, laughing at himself.

"It's a bit random though isn't it?" chipped in Sarah, Angela's friend.

"How do you mean?" Barker joined in.

"'Well, that's just it. It wasn't a fight, was it? A fight would happen spontaneously or be out of sight somewhere. This was very public. Like it was planned for effect or something."

Barker and Jared nodded.

"It'll give us all something to talk about when we get home."

Chapter 28

Barker ordered a couple of Martini's in the piano lounge after they'd left the restaurant.

"I've really enjoyed myself this evening, but it doesn't feel right somehow," said Lucy as took her first sip.

"Crazy day," Barker replied.

"Are you OK though John? Really?"

"'I'm fine. It's weird, I've been moping about for months but this has woken me up a bit, slapped me 'round the face maybe."

"Well thank you for this evening. It was a real change for me to do that."

"Back on duty tomorrow?"

"I assume so. Unless I hear otherwise. It's a sea-day, so everyone's onboard and we'll all be busy."

"In the Atrium?"

"Possibly, although I think I'm due on the Lido Deck soon. I'm not hard to find."

"No, I suppose not. I'm in room 9821 by the way. If you need me."

Lucy smiled. "I'll be in touch, don't you worry. We're a team now. Besides, I want to find out how that man is and let you know."

"I'm not optimistic," Barker said.

"No, but you never know."

VII

DAY EIGHT: AT SEA

Chapter 29

Barker's stateroom phone rang and woke him just after 8 am.

"John it's Lucy. Did I wake you?" a chirpy voice said.

"No. Well yes, but I should be up by now. I don't normally sleep this late," said Barker

"Sorry. Got some news though. The man who was shot is alive. 'Just a flesh wound,' the doctor said. I *think* he was joking. Anyway, the guy's seventy-two years old, so he's injured from the fall as much as anything else. Lots of bruises and a couple of fractures. Ruined his holiday but he'll live."

"Good. Any suspects?" asked Barker.

"Nothing official. I haven't spoken to Michael, but there are rumours. Something about a Latin American guy. Why he'd want to hurt an elderly ballroom dancer I've no idea."

"Back to work now?"

"Afraid so. I enjoyed that night off. I'll be here and there with the band all day. What about you?"

"I'm going to do as little as possible hopefully. A bit of reading by the pool or in a bar."

"Unlikely," said Lucy.

"What?"

"Unlikely that you'll sit around all day doing nothing. You're a policeman and there's been a crime. I've seen the movies."

"Not my jurisdiction. As they say in the movies."

"Whatever. I expect you to have solved it the next time I see you."

"Nothing to solve if they've caught the guy."

"No, but I can tell by the tone of your voice you don't think it's that simple do you?"

"Now who's the detective?"

"Actually, I have something else to tell you, but not on the phone."

"So when will I see you?"

Lucy paused, "Are you asking me out?"

Barker felt his face flush.

"No. you said you had something to tell me."

"So I did. I'm on in the lounge bar at five, just before the first dinner sitting? Forty-five minutes, then I've got an hour or so free."

"See you there," said Barker.

Chapter 30

Jaime Vega sat on the edge of a camp-bed in a six-by-six foot room with white plastic-clad walls, with nothing but a stainless steel sink and toilet bowl for company. On Galaxy Starlight this was what passed for a prison cell. There was a bright fluorescent strip light on the ceiling and a small window high up in the door, with a view onto the end of a corridor where nobody ever walked past unless they were coming to visit.

Vega was a petty criminal and odd job man for the cartels. He had joined Galaxy cruises through an agency in Manila, where most staff were recruited, as a kitchen porter. He'd done it on the advice of his boss who had been jailed after a deal went wrong. He'd told him it would be good regular money until he could get out and needed him again. Like everybody else, he worked hard and kept his head down, saving as much of his wage as he could to send back to his family living in what was little more than a three storey shed. There were a hundred and fifty others working in there with him, feeding three thousand rich, hungry westerners every day, but the camaraderie was good if you were good at your job. Sometimes things boiled over, tempers flared, but it was always quickly calmed down. It was a tight-knit group.

So when his boss resurfaced and offered him serious money to do a job, he saw a light at the end of the tunnel and thought about what it could do for his family, his kids. It could send them to school.

Vega was a small and wiry man with a mop of straight, dark, almost-black hair. Not big enough to look threatening, he scared people more with his attitude and was no stranger to a fight. He used to carry a gun but had rarely needed to use it apart from once, in a gang fight, out of self-defence. Negotiations went south and all hell let loose. He was armed. Everyone was. It was expected. Two of his friends were hit but survived. Two on the other side were killed, who knows how many injured. But he'd never done it in cold blood before.

The offer had come through a friend of his cousin working in kitchen prep. He thought about it for a day and then agreed. The cousin appeared that night with a pistol wrapped in kitchen cloths and hid it behind a microwave. The same spot he tried to hide it afterwards and got caught in the act.

On the day, he'd stolen a uniform from the laundry and wandered invisibly along to the Atrium, looking like just another bartender searching for customers. But he didn't stop to serve anyone. He circled the Atrium four or five times looking for his target and found a place between a pillar and a huge pot plant where he wouldn't be seen for the thirty seconds or so it would take.

After thinking about his escape route he found the target, straightened his arm, and aimed. That's when he'd started to shake. This was the first time he'd aimed a weapon at an unarmed person, a complete stranger. 'The money, Jaime, the money,' he'd thought. He closed his eyes, squeezed the trigger, and opened them after the pop.

One of the dancers circling the floor with his wife crashed onto the wood and glass table behind them, causing the others to scatter. Vega didn't have time to wait and see what happened next. He did the only thing he could do, and walked away, taking full advantage of the distraction.

An hour and a half later, he ended up in a cell.

Chapter 31

Dressed for dinner in dark trousers, white shirt and a grey sports jacket, Barker found himself a seat in a quiet corner of the Navigators Lounge on Deck Seven just aft of the Atrium. He'd walked in through the entrance on the port side of the ship but deliberately crossed the empty dance floor in front of the band to the opposite side of the room so that Lucy would notice where he was heading. He didn't look in her direction in case that was too obvious, but recognised the sound of her voice, quieter this afternoon in front of the few people who didn't want to be out in the sun on the Lido Deck.

One bottle of cheap American beer later the singing stopped and a polite round of applause was followed by a word of thanks from Lucy, letting them know where she would be singing again this evening. She left the stage in the opposite direction to where Barker was sat, and for a moment he thought she'd forgotten him. She walked out of the door he'd come in, but circled around the casino next door and came back in on his side, smiling.

Dressed relatively casually, she walked between a few other chairs and tables to get to the back of the room where Barker sat facing the stage. Her favourite perfume reached his nose before Lucy pulled a chair up close to him, and said, "So what's new?"

Barker smiled and waved at a passing waiter, who walked over and took their order. "Nothing much."

"Did you manage to do nothing all day?" Lucy asked.

"Isn't that what you're supposed to do on cruises?"

"I guess so. Lucky for some."

"What's the internet like on here?" Barker asked.

"Expensive."

"Fast?"

"Hmm. So, so. A bit like normal broadband but not fibre fast. I get an hour a day free. What do you want to do?"

"Oh, I just need to do some homework. Look a few people up. I don't want to use up your allowance."

"Oh, I hardly use it. A couple of emails a week to my Mum and that's it."

"Boyfriend?" asked Barker.

"Not since I went home early nine months ago and found my best friend on top of him in our bed, no."

"Oh crap, sorry."

"Better off without them both, obviously."

Before Barker could reply, he noticed the figure of a tall, olive-skinned woman with dark brown hair halfway down her back slinking towards them in the aisle between the chairs, wearing a classic LBD and black heels. Barker stared for a little too long and caught her eye as she passed. Was there a hint of a smile? Lucy noticed his distraction and turned her head to see what he was looking at.

"Story of my life," she said. "Better looking woman walks in and distracts the man I'm with. Anyway, wasn't that..."

"Maria Cortez." Barker blurted, involuntarily.

"You know her name? Fast work John. Should I be jealous?"

101

"I followed her yesterday." Barker continued, still distracted.

"Woah, you're going to have to explain that," said Lucy.

John sighed. "I'm here to watch her."

"No kidding," replied Lucy.

"No, I mean, I've been sent by a friend in the police force to keep an eye on her."

"Why?"

"Don't know. I mean, they won't tell me anything except she went missing and then reappeared out of nowhere. They won't tell me what she's done."

"Jeez, so I was right about you?" Lucy said.

"What do you mean?"

"I mean all this 'nothing' you've been doing – it's a sham."

"No. There's nothing to do is there?' She can't go anywhere. All I'm supposed to do is watch what she does and who she associates with. I've seen her for a total of about fifteen minutes on the whole trip."

"Chat her up," Lucy said out of the blue.

"What?"

"Chat her up. That way you'll get to know what she's up to."

"Or what cover story she's dreamt up," Barker replied. "Besides, I'm crap at that."

"Well I'm here aren't I?" Lucy smiled mischievously.

"I didn't chat you up. You chatted me up!" said Barker.

"I did not!"

"I threw a drink over you and you came back and chatted me up."

"I thought the drink thing was your way of introducing yourself. But of course you were staring at Maria in her swimsuit, so I should have known better." Lucy giggled at

Barker squirming.

Barker looked at Lucy, shook his head and gave her a wry smile. "You drive me mad."

Chapter 32

Boredom was eating away at Vega now, but he knew this was the calm before the storm. A murder charge would take him away from his family for a long time. He'd been an idiot. He'd hoped to change his kids' lives, and he had, but in the opposite way to how he'd intended. Now they wouldn't even see his cruise ship wages. He'd be lucky if his wife stayed with him. The kids would be grown up by the time he got out, probably in the same gangs he'd got dragged into, with no way of preventing it.

He felt the urge to use the toilet and despite the handcuffs, managed to pull his pants down and sit on the bowl. No sooner had he sat down than he heard footsteps in the corridor outside. A few seconds passed before he heard anything at the lock.

"Hey, I'm on the toilet man, give me a minute!" he shouted.

There was no answer and no face at the window. The lock clicked and the door handle moved.

"Gimme a bit of privacy will you?!"

The door opened slowly. Vega looked up from the inter-loper's feet to their face and locked eyes. "Come on, I...what?"

Vega tried to stand but was pushed down by a gloved hand on his head as the intruder stepped into the tiny room. A second gloved hand sank a narrow blade into his chest and blood bubbled up in his throat. The knife was withdrawn and plunged back in straight through his heart. Vega slumped to the floor, pants around his ankles. The intruder dropped the knife, turned, and walked out, quietly clicking the door shut on the way.

Chapter 33

"You said you had something to tell me," Barker said, changing the subject.

"What? Oh, I did, didn't I?" Lucy replied, "It may be nothing. It's just something I overheard in the medical centre."

"Go on."

"Well I can't remember the exact words, but the gist of what I heard the crew talking about was that they'd been pretty busy and had more than one fatality already on this cruise and were glad this wasn't another one."

"Right."

"You're not easily impressed are you?" said Lucy.

"Just more used to dead people than you. Carry on."

"Well, that's it really."

"Nothing else?"

"Well, something about a heart attack in the gym or the restaurant."

"Doesn't that happen on cruises all the time though? What with the average age being so high? There must be loads of passengers with dodgy tickers."

"Well, you do see someone carried out of the bar or restaurant on a stretcher now and then, but I never really find out what happened to them."

"Any hint of foul play?"

"Foul play? Who are you, Sherlock Holmes?"

"Funny. Did they think there was anything suspicious about the other deaths?"

"Not that I could tell." Lucy concluded, disappointed. "There was that accident when we stopped in Gibraltar as well, but that wasn't on board ship."

"What happened?"

"Road accident, so I heard."

"Doesn't sound like your average serial killer does it?" Barker said, failing to hide a hint of sarcasm.

"I just thought it might be useful to know, that's all"

"Can you find out more?" Barker asked.

"More what? Bodies?"

"More *about* the bodies. Like who they were? Can you access the manifest?"

"The what fest?"

"The passenger manifest. A list of all the passengers. We need to find out who they were."

"I can't myself. I'm not crew. I know a lot of the crew but I don't have any access to stuff like that."

"Do you know anyone who could get in for you?"

"There's Igor on the guest relations desk I suppose. He's a sweetie. He's my GBF."

"Igor? Really? What's a GBF?"

"Yes, Igor. Gay Best Friend. But it's not much fun being gay in Russia, so he ran away to sea."

"And he likes you?"

"Yes. He'll help me, but I can't get him into any trouble."

"No, no. Just see if he can use the system to find out who died. I mean it probably won't say 'deceased' on there, but it might have some notes about staterooms, and names. It will show if anyone got off the ship at any point. You know, in a bag or something."

"Nice. OK, I'll see if I can speak to him when I'm passing, but it will have to be if he's on a late shift. It's way too busy in the daytime to be asking about dead bodies. Are you going to finish that drink?"

Lucy took a sip from her mineral water, almost choked, and spat, 'Eric Spencer.'

"What?" said Barker, looking startled and wiping his face.

"That's the man who was shot. That's your homework. Google him while I go and chat up Igor."

Chapter 34

Rebecca Collins stood at the arrivals barrier in Funchal airport shaking and holding back the tears that she knew would flow when her in-laws walked through the door a few meters in front of her. Her own parents had died years before and her sister lived in Melbourne, Australia. Dave's parents Trevor and Diane had booked a flight as soon as she'd told them the news of his death over the phone the day before. Their flight had landed ten minutes ago, and as they were only coming to help her pick up Dave's body for its return to the UK, they would not be waiting at the carousel for any baggage.

All around her, Rebecca watched excited faces arriving for their holidays, picking up coaches and taxis and looking for information desks, plus a few locals arriving home and being greeted by family. Just another day in an airport for everyone but her. Two familiar faces soon appeared in the crowd, distinguished from everyone else by red eyes and no smiles. Rebecca couldn't hold on any longer. As they reached the barrier and leaned over to hug her, the tears came to her and Diane. Trevor did his best to hold back, being of the generation where men don't cry, but it was obvious that he had done so in the last twenty-four hours.

Their hugs went on silently for a good minute or so before

Rebecca managed, "Let's get out. I can't stand it in here. There's a taxi outside waiting to take us to the hospital."

The three members of the Collins family trudged outside into the warm evening and climbed wearily into the waiting car.

Chapter 35

Barker decided against dining in the main restaurant and went to the Lido Deck into the Skyscape restaurant. It was usually a lot calmer and quieter at this time of day as the majority were eating downstairs. He grabbed a plate and helped himself to some grilled fish and rice and vegetables and sat down by the window watching the sun go down.

After about twenty minutes, he finished his meal and decided to find the ship's Internet Café. Once found in every city these places were as rare as hen's teeth now, except on cruise ships, where the middle-aged clientele were unlikely to have brought their own laptop and were too long-sighted to be able to use the internet on their smartphone, if they had one.

He found the iCafe on Deck Six and ordered a decaf tea and a couple of cookies and grabbed a spare seat in front of a pretty new PC with a touchscreen. There were half a dozen other people in there with him, plus a few empty seats. He typed in the ID and password Lucy had scribbled on the beer mat at their table and logged on. Google popped up as the home page and he typed 'Eric Spencer' into the box. There were a couple of Facebook entries and one for LinkedIn, but those were profiles of men younger than the one currently in Starlight's medical centre. Being around seventy years old he was less likely to be found online than someone ten or twenty years younger, unless he was rich, famous, or notorious.

This was something Barker ought to be good at and he refused to give up so soon. After another twenty minutes of digging he came across an Eric Spencer mentioned in a PDF stored on a website. Clicking on it brought up a newsletter of an accountancy practice – Spencer and Simpson - whose eldest partner Eric Spencer, ex-Royal Navy officer, had retired a couple of months ago.

Barker's memory of the man whom he'd last seen lying on the Atrium floor was a bit hazy, but it was definitely him. He looked perfectly ordinary, perfectly boring. Not the sort of man to have a price on his head. Why should he bother digging anymore? What did this have to do with Maria Cortez? She was the reason he was on the ship in the first place. Unless this was anything to do with that, why should he make more work for himself? He tapped a few names and dates and company details into a blank memo on his phone and clicked away to check his personal emails and drink his tea.

Chapter 36

Igor was a handsome young man and perfectly groomed. Lucy thought she detected a bit of eyeliner occasionally when he thought he could get away with it. He was loving life on board ship where he could be himself, unlike back in his hometown where he'd been bullied and abused almost daily. He hated the thought of having to go back.

He was a hit with the passengers too, women mostly of course. There were still a few elderly men who stumbled a bit when they spoke to him, as if they didn't know how to communicate with a gay man properly, like they speak a different language. Igor noticed it but never made a fuss. It was nothing compared to what he'd grown up with, and here he was in a position of authority.

"Lucy! What are you doing here? Not singing?" Igor said as he saw her approach.

"Not right now, Igor. How are you?" Lucy replied as she gave him a hug at the end of the long, semi-circular Guest Relations counter. Igor was a hugger. Lucy liked that. He always smelled so good. In a parallel universe she might have been attracted to him if he only had a bit more meat on his bones. She shuddered at the thought of her last boyfriend, and Michael – both perfect specimens – and how those relationships had gone south.

"We have to go dancing,' said Igor, 'in Sky Bar one night time."

"Yes, we will, I promise."

"You keep saying that!"

"I know, I'm sorry. We will soon."

"Maybe. Maybe. Is this social visit?"

Lucy grinned apologetically, "Not exactly."

"Ah! You see, you want something from me."

"I do. It's a weird one. You remember the guy that was shot at in the Atrium the other day?"

"Yes, yes. He's OK. He's fine. Well he's not fine but he didn't die."

"I know, I know. But I've heard rumours about other casualties on this cruise, more than normal. Can you help me find out who they were?"

"Why?' said Igor, 'Why you need to know this? Don't security team know?"

"I'm sure they do, but I don't know whether they're doing anything about it. And I met this friend..."

"What friend?"

"Just a man. A policeman. He wants to see if we can find out who the other people are, the ones who have left the ship because they've...died. Can you find that out? Do you have a list?"

Igor looked puzzled for a few seconds then said, "I can check passenger list. Compare it to original, see who left. But it would take hours. We have three thousand passenger."

"Hmm, never thought of that," said Lucy, disappointed.

"But maybe I can see who is admitted to Medical Centre. Much quicker. Leave it with me. I get back to you. Now when we go partying?"

"Oh soon, soon. I promise."

VIII

DAY NINE: AT SEA

Chapter 37

The next morning the Lido Deck was basking in the best weather of the cruise so far as Starlight headed west towards the Caribbean. There was a Disney film showing on the big screen at one end, but not all the kids were watching it as the pool itself was almost full of them. At the other end the bar staff were serving beer and cocktails to people in swimming costumes who sat on bar stools or tottered off to find their significant other on their sun loungers on either side of the pool and dotted in between. Fully-dressed people weaved their way through from their staterooms to the Skyscape restaurant for a late breakfast or early lunch – hard to define in a twenty-four-seven restaurant environment.

Despite the advice to stay out of the midday sun the loungers were usually occupied by this time, or at least reserved with a towel and a paperback, and their owners in the pool or the bar. People who would never drink alcohol nor bask in the sun at this time of day somehow felt happy to do so on holiday, away from disapproving friends and neighbours.

Samantha Howard had been lucky. She'd arrived only half an hour ago and managed to find two free loungers together for herself and her husband Jonathan, who had soon got bored and gone for a wander around the decks, looking for anything he might have missed in his first few days. She knew he wouldn't be long, so she settled down with her book and her Pina Colada and fleetingly remembered her stressful nursing job, and how nice it was to not have to worry about it for another week.

If she hadn't lifted the cocktail glass to her mouth and taken a sip through the curly straw, Samantha might have survived the impact of the thirteen-stone body that fell on her from the deck above with just a few broken bones and some internal bleeding. But the stem of the plastic glass that was designed not to break if it fell over on the deck sheared completely off under the sudden force, and the remainder was pushed down below her sternum into her belly, rupturing intestines and causing massive bleeding.

The plastic sun lounger failed to cushion any of the blow and split across the middle and gave up one of its side legs. Samantha and the man who had unknowingly killed her slid off the lounger onto the deck, into the gap between her lounger and the next.

There was a brief moment of calm when all the movement stopped, apart from Samantha's mouth opening in a silent scream, and her head tilting down to look at the body sliding off her abdomen onto her legs, exposing her bloody wound. As she turned her head sideways instinctively to look for help from her husband, the first screams began, and the sound of dragging sun loungers being moved out of the way.

The screams weren't just for Samantha, but due to the sight of the stubby handle of a stiletto knife sticking out of the man's neck and for the sheer amount of blood the two of them were releasing onto the deck.

"Move back, move back," said a man in blue shorts who had grabbed a couple of rolled-up towels from the store by the pool and knew the only thing he could do was to try to stem the blood flow. As he handed one towel to another man stood nearest to the knife victim and stepped through to Samantha's side, the onlookers slowly shuffled back.

"Is anybody a nurse or a doctor?" said the man as he un-folded the towel slightly and laid it over Samantha's stomach, unsure how to apply pressure to a wound with shards of plastic in it. The other man fought his instinct to pull the knife out of the faller's neck so he could cover the wound. He was sure he'd heard you shouldn't do that in case it made things worse. Or had he? In the end he just wrapped the towel as closely around the knife as he could and watched it soak up the gushing blood.

"I have called the medical centre sir," said a voice approach-ing from the bar area, "Please, everybody, move away. Lido Deck is closed. Please move."

Remembering their children, mothers ran to gather them up and usher them away, with the soundtrack of the Disney film still singing in the background. Others gasped in shock and the conversation level grew with people discussing who had seen what. Drinks were knocked over as people moved distractedly away from the scene and a group of people, part passengers, part staff, grabbed towels and held them up around the bodies as if to protect what remained of their dignity. As if they knew that was the last decent thing they could do for them both.

On the deck above, people climbed off their loungers and moved towards the railings for a view over the pool. One person moved in the other direction, calmly and quietly away from the scene, blending in with the crowds as if nothing unusual was going on.

Chapter 38

In the Skyscape restaurant at the back of the ship on the same deck as the swimming pool, Barker was sitting by a window eating a late breakfast and gazing out at the blazing sun reflecting off the Atlantic Ocean, dimmed a little by the heavily-tinted floor-to-ceiling glass. It was always noisy and slightly chaotic in there, but the volume crept up when a flurry of people wandered in from the pool end of the restaurant, talking loudly and moving about trying to find somewhere to sit. He noticed they weren't going straight for the food as they normally would, but just finding places to sit down. The numbers kept growing and it was obvious they'd been ushered in by staff when the large fire doors separating the restaurant from the pool were closed behind them.

As people passed him Barker caught random words from hurried conversations - 'awful', 'blood everywhere', 'must be dead', 'poor woman' – not enough to make any sense, but enough to tell him something bad had happened. Again.

He got up and refilled his mug with coffee from the nearby drinks station and sat down again to wait for the place to settle, watching closely and absorbing the atmosphere to get a feel for who he could ask about what had gone on. A lot of people were babbling and jabbering and asking each other if they'd 'seen it happen'. Some children had obviously been crying. Barker picked up pieces of events by listening and taking it all in.

"Is anybody sitting here?" said a voice from his left side. It came from an elderly man who was holding his wife's hand, hoping to sit opposite Barker at the table-for-four he currently had to himself.

"No, please," said Barker gesturing at the empty seats, "Has something happened?" he asked.

"It was horrible," the woman said, "Horrible. He just fell. I heard a crunch and then everybody started screaming."

"Who fell?" asked Barker.

"A man fell from the deck above," the old man joined in, "Onto a woman on a sun lounger. Then there was blood. He had something sticking out of his neck. Neither of them moved."

"I saw it," said the woman, "I was reading my book, facing that direction. I saw something drop. Didn't realise what it was until the commotion. What on earth is going wrong with this cruise? Why are all these things happening? Somebody has to do something."

"I'll get some tea," said the man as he stood up and shuffled off to the drinks station, leaving his distressed wife to chat to Barker for another few minutes. When he came back, Barker reassured them that the crew would get things under control and made his excuses and left the restaurant. Normally he would have walked past the pool, but this time he had no choice but to head out to the rear of the ship where a lot of the other passengers were gathered, sharing their versions of events.

Barker knew that he had to take advantage of the confusion

to find out more information before everything got 'locked down' and kept quiet. The security staff would soon be in control and release a statement to calm everybody down and try to prevent further speculation. Now was the best time to investigate. Maybe if everyone was focused on this incident, they wouldn't be thinking too much about previous ones and he could use the distraction to his advantage. He needed to find a pattern to these events that might lead him to a suspect or at least prevent further attacks. But he couldn't do it alone.

Chapter 39

Jonathan Howard had never been much of a reader. Consequently, he couldn't lie on a sun lounger for long. There's only so much people-watching you can do, and he was a bit self-conscious at that. He thought it strange that it seemed fine to nosy at what other people were doing when dressed in skimpy clothes and all crammed next to one another in rows by a noisy pool. Well, you didn't nosy at the person next to you of course, that would be weird. But you could nosy at people walking past or on the other side of the pool, or on the deck above. It was kind of accepted that it was OK because everyone was doing it. It's amazing how people's inhibitions get put on hold on holiday, he thought. Imagine if he'd suggested an office party in underwear – which is basically what the Lido Deck was? He'd be dragged straight to Human Resources and booked on a course about inappropriate behaviour within minutes. Well, he would if he wasn't the director of Human resources.

So he got up, smiled at his wife, and said, "I'm going for a walk."

"OK" she replied, without looking up from her book and cocktail.

They were relaxed like that, him and Samantha. They'd been together twelve years, married for seven, two children and a cockapoo at home being looked after by grandparents. They didn't mind each other having their own space. They'd met at work, she had been his boss for a year until she became operations director – a bit of a switch, but she'd been at the company a lot longer than him and knew it inside out.

He looked around before deciding which way to go and took the easiest way out of the maze of loungers and abandoned plastic drinks glasses waiting to be collected by the bartenders, and headed for the nearest staircase up to the next deck. Deck Seventeen had a big gap in it above the Lido Deck, so he wandered over to the port side and looked out over the railings at the endless expanse of Atlantic Ocean. Very nice, he thought, but after a few minutes contemplation he wandered along the deck and turned left under the large video screen belting out the afternoon's entertainment. He could see Samantha from here, but it was too loud to hang around, so he carried on and turned left again in a circuit that would take him back to where he started. There were lots of people around on sun loungers angled towards the screen, plus a few crew members and cleaners wandering around. A passing bartender asked, "Drink sir?" to which he replied, "No, thank you."

At the opposite end to the screen, there was a raised area used for the bands that played at intervals each day. Lucy something was one of them, he remembered, quite good she was, very pretty too. The stage was empty right now and there was no room for sun loungers. He turned around to face the video screen and watched for a minute or two until he felt an arm slip around the left side of his waist and a body pressing into him from his right side as if in some sort of sideways hug. As he turned his head to see who it was, there was a blinding pain in the right side of his neck and a firm but simple push in

126

his back that lifted him over the railings he'd been leaning on. The last thing he heard before he killed his wife was, 'Let it go, let it go!'

Chapter 40

That's how it should be done. Calmly and clinically. Pick the right spot, where nobody is looking and wait for him to walk around, use the knife – the right choice I think – and tip him over the railing. In truth he pretty much fell over it himself with the shock, he didn't need much help.

And two for one was genius. I wonder if she knew in the last few seconds that her husband had killed her?

Chapter 41

Lucy was in her stateroom getting ready for her mid-day appearance on the Lido Deck when the phone rang. It was a message to tell her that her shift was cancelled because of a 'security incident'.

"What does that mean?" she asked the caller.

"I can't say," replied the voice.

"Come on Caitlin, what happened?" asked Lucy, recognising the caller from the staff office.

"I don't know for certain Lucy. I heard there was a fight, someone got stabbed. But it's pretty serious if they've closed the deck. Medical have gone, all the first aiders, and the security staff."

"And that's it? Just the Lido Deck?"

"So far yes. There might be more but that's all I know right now."

"OK mate, thanks. Let me know if you find anything out."

Lucy put the phone down and changed back into shorts and a t-shirt, putting away the outfit she'd planned to wear, when there was a knock at the door. She opened it to find Barker stood outside, frowning.

"This is becoming a habit," he said. "Fancy a coffee?"

"I'd rather have a cocktail and some sun."

Chapter 42

Months of experience had taught Lucy where to find the sheltered spots on deck that didn't get the full force of the wind when the ship was mid-ocean. There were plenty if you knew where to look, usually higher up above the Lido Deck and further away from the bars, where it was harder to get the attention of a passing waiter hoping to sell you a drink. The middle of the ship below the funnels was always empty because of the noise of the exhausts sucking fumes out of the bowels of the ship. Lucy and Barker found a couple of loungers in a corner not too close to other people and sat down with the drinks they'd picked up at the bar on the deck below. Barker hadn't said much on the walk up, general chit-chat mostly, not wanting to discuss was what on his mind too publicly. But then that's what all the other passengers were doing.

"Another one bites the dust," he said grimly.

"Is that police humour?" said Lucy.

"Sorry. Shouldn't be so casual about it, but it's getting silly now."

"Were you there? I heard there was a fight."

"No, I was having breakfast. People told me someone fell onto the Lido Deck. Onto a woman on a lounger."

"Jeez, that's bad luck."

"I don't know if luck's got much to do with it. This all feels more and more planned. We need to do some digging. Can you help me find out who any of these people are?"

"Maybe. I spoke to Igor yesterday. He said he'll try to get names from the medical records. I don't know how he's going to do that. I don't want him getting sacked. Where do we start?"

"Well, security will be all over these two right now, so let's leave them alone and try to get at the others. Find out who they were."

"And then what?"

"Can we get in their rooms? Can you get hold of a master key or whatever?"

"Shit, John, you don't want much do you? How am I going to do that?"

"I don't know Lucy but we have to try. We've got five more days on this ship and there could be more people at risk if we don't work out what's going on."

"What about back home? Haven't you heard anything from your boss? Have you managed to tell him what's going on?" Lucy asked.

"Nothing. I managed to get hold of him a few days ago but wouldn't tell me anything. Ever since then the satellite signal's been patchy – we're in the middle of the ocean I guess – so I've emailed him to keep him up to date.' Barker replied. 'What about you? Shouldn't you be working?"

"Yep, on the Lido Deck, right now."

"Ah, OK," said Barker.

"I'm on in the Wheelhouse bar later but I'd expect to be shuffled around when they start to rearrange things."

"What do you mean?"

131

"Well, I reckon they'll want to demonstrate that they're in control of the situation and close a few places, even if it just makes the passengers feel a bit better. Otherwise there's going to be a lot of nervous people around making life harder. A friend in the security team said that's what they sometimes do."

"Hmmm, so it might get harder to move around the ship?"

"I guess so."

"We'd better get moving then. Can we go and find your friend Igor?"

Chapter 43

Rebecca Collins was at the Dr. Nelio Mendonca hospital in Funchal with her in-laws Trevor and Diane, where they had spent most of the morning. There seemed to be so much time to wait and paperwork to complete, when all they wanted to do was take David home. Diane was inconsolable at the death of her only child. Trevor was stunned and said very little. They had asked Rebecca several times what had happened, but she only knew what the ship's staff had told her – that David's body had been found at the end of a treadmill by a woman who had been using a cross-trainer in the opposite corner of the room. She hadn't known how long he'd been there as she was wearing headphones, but she guessed it was only a few minutes as she changed machines regularly and thought she would have noticed otherwise. Starlight's medical staff had briefly examined David, but could only assume he'd had a heart attack as there were no obvious wounds on his body.

"But he didn't have a heart condition," Diane said, "Did he?" she continued, looking at Trevor.

"No, no. Fit as a fiddle, David." Trevor replied, staring blankly into space.

"I know Diane, but these things can be hidden. It can just happen," said Rebecca calmly. She'd had an extra day to start to comes to terms with David's death and was trying to keep it together at least until she got home.

"What did he eat the night before? Could it have been that?" Diane questioned Rebecca again.

"No Diane, I can't remember, I think it was fish probably."

"Seafood? That can be bad, can't it? Allergies."

"Yes, possibly, but I think we'd have known sooner than the following morning. And I don't think fish is that bad. Mussels maybe. Anyway, I'm sure they're going to tell us sooner or later."

Rebecca wished Diane would stop speculating. She just wanted peace. Her head ached with grief, but at the same time she didn't want to be alone. She wanted David. She wanted to get him home so she could grieve properly at the home they'd shared for twelve years. But she understood how bad Diane and Trevor must feel to have lost their son, even though they'd not had any of their own.

"Oh, I saw Sam and Jordan on the ship, had a quick chat one day," said Rebecca, trying to change the subject."

"Sam & Jordan? Remind me," said Diane.

"You know Sam, Graham's daughter, and her husband Jordan."

"Oh, the Smithsons? Really? That's a coincidence. Did they have the kids with them?"

"No, left them with the grandparents. Won two tickets apparently, just for the two of them. I suppose they could have paid to take the kids, but they've not had a holiday on their own for years, so they took the opportunity."

"They deserve it. Sam works hard. So Graham says anyway. Graham wants her to come and work for us, but I don't think she's too keen."

"Oh, and I saw another couple that looked familiar but I couldn't place them. Dave said they might be from your place, but I don't know. Maybe I've met them on Christmas parties."

"What did they look like?"

"Tall man, young-ish. Well, in his late thirties maybe. I spotted his wife first, in the dining room, very beautiful, and long red hair. I didn't go and talk to them though because I wasn't sure what to say. Maybe if we'd been there longer..."

"Mitchell. Jack Mitchell. And his wife Katie. Yes, she is very pretty" replied Diane.

A woman wearing a white coat and carrying a clipboard walked around the corner into the corridor where they were waiting and said, "Mrs Collins? Rebecca Collins? Could you come with me please?"

Chapter 44

Igor was on the front desk printing. He had been asked to print a letter from the captain and head of security about their reaction to the incident by the pool. He had to print enough copies to hand out to the dozens...hundreds of people who were popping by to ask that very question. The sooner he got them done he would just have to hand out a leaflet instead. Much less stressful.

As he was helping a customer he saw Lucy in the queue with John in tow. Once he'd finished with the elderly woman who'd seemingly lost her marbles, he waved at Lucy to come to the end of the desk.

Lucy and Barker walked over to Igor looking like a couple of queue-jumpers.

"Igor, this is John. He's a policeman...in England," said Lucy.

"Hi John," Igor smiled at Barker, "You are the man Lucy keeps talking about?"

"Stop it Igor. Can you help me with what we talked about yesterday? What's this?" Lucy said, pointing to the sheets coming out of the printer.

"Ah, this is from Captain. New rules. Curfew. I have to give out to guests who come here. You will get one in your room later."

"Can I read one now?" John asked.

"Sure," Igor replied and slid a copy across the table towards Lucy along with a plain envelope. He looked directly at her and Lucy got the impression he wanted her to take it and not ask any more questions.

"We'll need a key," Lucy whispered, looking at Igor pleadingly. But Igor wasn't impressed, shook his head and walked back to his customers.

Chapter 45

Lucy had been right about the security measures being put in place, but even she hadn't expected them to go so far. There was to be a curfew at midnight for all passengers, and fixed dining times – two sittings – instead of having the choice of going at any time you liked. The machines normally used to scan people on and off the ship in ports would be used to monitor who was in the dining rooms, the main theatre and certain bars, the spa, the gym etc. Other public areas would be restricted as and when necessary. And the Skyscape restaurant would no longer be 24/7. Lucy knew that this didn't mean that security had any clue what was going on, but it was an attempt to make it seem like they were in control. It would reassure people that they were safe and being watched over. Whether it would work was anyone's guess.

"What's in the envelope?" said Barker?

Lucy looked down and picked up the envelope that Igor had given her off the table they were sat by in the coffee shop. She said nothing, glanced up at Barker and slid her finger under the flap and opened it up. She unfolded the A4 sheet to find only two lines printed on it...

Mitchell 10244
Gibson 13118

"That's not much," Lucy said, disappointed.

"I've seen worse," said Barker. "It gives us names, that's a start."

"So now what?"

"I'll think of something. I'll be in touch after you've finished work."

Chapter 46

Around 7.15 p.m. Barker walked into Starlight's main theatre at the very front of the ship and struggled to make sense of the scale of it. Apart from some parts of the Atrium it was the only space inside the ship that spanned its entire width. He stood to one side of the starboard-side staircase on the top floor of three and looked down at the stairways, aisles and row upon row of seats, enough for around a thousand people. It was hard to believe you could be inside a ship. It just didn't seem possible to have a full-size theatre floating around in the middle of the ocean. He hadn't been in before because musicals weren't really his thing, but tonight there was a tribute artist on who he thought he might like and the new security measures were limiting people's options for using the other public spaces, so it was going to be packed. He'd arrived fifteen minutes before the show was due to begin but the theatre was already half full and passengers were streaming through behind him. He thought he ought to find a seat before they all filled up and walked down the aisle a few steps, looking for a row he could join.

He found a row on his left that was filling up and sat down next to a group of four adults, leaving a few spare seats on his right-hand side for others to fill. The anticipation was building and the noise of people chatting was loud enough to be distracting. He looked around at the decor and the lighting rigs in front of the stage and at the different types of people walking in: mostly middle-aged, middle-class Europeans and Americans, talking about the events of the past day or two. He didn't know whether this atmosphere was typical or whether it was because of the nature of the events of the past week.

The lights in the theatre went down slightly but there was still ten minutes to go before the show started. Barker felt a presence on his right side – someone filling the seat immediately next to him. A light perfume wafted over him and he turned to make a polite smile of acknowledgement as his neighbour settled into her seat. His heart bounced inside his chest as he found his smile returned by Maria Cortez, fragrant and beautiful, crossing her legs and putting her small black patent-leather clutch bag under her seat

"Good evening," she said, in a soft, husky, Spanish-accent, looking right into his eyes.

"Evening," Barker replied, wondering how much his expression had given away his nervousness, his heart still pounding at twice the normal rate. Breathe slowly, he thought, don't make a fool of yourself. Look around, don't make a big deal. What's the problem?

"I knew it would be packed in here," said Maria, "It's always popular, but especially now."

Barker turned back and looked to see Maria facing him, obviously expecting to strike up a conversation, rather than just making a throwaway comment.

"Yes," he said nervously. "I've not been in before."

"Really?! It's my favourite place on the ship. Such an escape. So different from everyday life."

Maria turned towards Barker and leaned on the shared armrest between them, her legs crossed towards him. Given an excuse to look directly at her, Barker was taken aback by just how beautiful she was. Intimidatingly so. Long, almost-black hair, dark brown eyes, olive-skinned, probably 5ft 10 inches tall without the four-inch black heels she was wearing. Her long black dress had thin straps revealing her shoulders and arms, and her legs came out of the long slit down the left side. His wife Laura was an attractive woman but Maria Cortez was like a supermodel and he felt like an awkward teenager talking to the most popular girl in school.

"Where are you from?" said Barker. Standard small talk but maybe he'd also get some information.

"Colombia," Maria replied, "and you?"

"London," said Barker, "But I live in Spain now."

"Oh wow, Spain! I've never been, believe it or not."

"It's a bit too hot for me. I'm not used to it yet."

"Oh, I love the heat. You'll love it once you're used to it," said Maria, looking away and scanning the theatre in front of them. "They've handled it well don't you think?" said Maria, nodding towards the stage.

"Sorry?" Barker replied.

"The passengers. They've handled the changes well. The new schedule, the security restrictions. I wondered how it would go down, but there's been no trouble I think."

"Well it's my first cruise," said Barker, "So I don't know what they're normally like. But I guess it's given people a lot to talk about. Everyone is very animated."

Barely perceptibly the lights started to dim and the chatter began to subside before a sharp-suited twenty-something bounded on to the stage to introduce the evening's entertainment. Maria turned and flashed another smile at Barker before settling back in her seat to watch the show.

Chapter 47

Clifford was from a suburb of Manila, capital of the Philippines. He'd been on Starlight since she was launched and three other ships before that. He was one of the more experienced stateroom stewards and was hoping for a promotion at the end of his current contract. His family could do with the money – it would mean he could continue sending his children to school and pay for a few extras. He had spent the last hour turning down beds in his guest's rooms. As he passed room 3363 he looked around and bent down as if to pick up a loose bit of litter on the floor, and slipped a blank silver disc underneath the door.

Inside room 3363 Lucy was getting undressed after her last appearance of the day, putting her dress on a hanger in the wardrobe. She noticed the disc on the floor and wondered how long it had been there. It was identical in size and shape to the Sea Stars that opened the stateroom doors but the only marking on it was a solitary five-pointed star in the centre.

"Good man Igor!" she whispered, smiling to herself, "John will be pleased."

Chapter 48

In the theatre, the applause began to subside after the encore and guests sat back down in their seats to listen to a thank you from the cruise director. The lights slowly brightened and Barker remembered he was on a ship and sat next to Maria Cortez, whom he felt obliged to resume his conversation with now that the show had ended.

"That was really good. I'm glad I came tonight," he said shyly as he turned to face her.

"Yes it was," Maria replied as she retrieved her handbag and looked at the growing queue of people in the aisle making their way up the stairs past her toward the exits. Her smile changed into a look of friendly concern. She looked into Barker's eyes and said, "Listen John. You're a nice guy. You don't need to get involved in this."

"How...How do you know my name?" Barker stuttered, heart bouncing all over again.

"The same way you know my name John - homework. Look, please keep out of things that you don't understand. They will hurt the ones closest to you. You of all people should know that." Maria continued, and in one slick movement she stood up, turned to her right, and stepped into the queue of people leaving the theatre, striding up a couple of steps and squeezing between people to put distance between them.

Barker slumped back stunned in his seat. He could have convinced himself he'd misheard most of it, but that last sentence, 'You of all people should know that.' That was aimed directly at him. What the hell did that mean? Who is Maria Cortez and why would she say that?

He could have stayed put and got his breath back but that last comment lit a fire under him and he jumped up out of his seat and pushed his way into the queueing theatre-goers on the stairs, earning a few tuts from an elderly couple he squeezed in front of. He could just see Maria leaving through the doors at the top of the staircase.

''Scuse me. Excuse me please," Barker said as he nudged his way past the people immediately in front. 'I'm not very well,' he said, putting his hand over his mouth as if he was about to vomit. Four people in front turned and saw him and backed off, not wanting to get their expensive clothes covered in whatever this drunkard had eaten for dinner.

But Maria had disappeared when he got to the top of the staircase and out of the doors. He couldn't see her in front of him amongst the crowd of people intent on filling the nearest bar. But she wouldn't be so naïve as to walk straight on would she, if she was avoiding being followed? The only way she could have turned was right, over to the port side of the ship, then left to continue towards the Atrium.

Or maybe she went down the staircase behind him? Down a deck or two to quickly get out of sight. No, Barker thought, that would leave her on her own and exposed if he happened to guess correctly. Better to stay in a crowd where she was protected and he couldn't catch her as quickly. So he turned left and followed the crowd of people leaving the theatre from the other side of the ship, heading towards the top deck of the Atrium through the wine bar, where a lot of people would stop for a drink before the eleven o'clock curfew came into effect.

Barker quickened his step as the crowd began to thin out and gaps appeared. He could be completely mistaken, but if he guessed right he was sure he would catch Maria up. As he exited the other side of the wine bar he caught a glimpse of a tall, dark-haired woman descending the staircase in the Atrium down the middle level. It must be her. He didn't see her face properly, but Maria was so distinctive and unlike any of the other passengers, it had to be her.

He skipped between a family walking around the Atrium balcony and found the staircase heading down. Maria was another floor below, heading for the lowest deck of the Atrium. As Barker got down the first flight of stairs he glanced over the handrail to his left and saw Maria's heels just disappearing into one of the corridors leading to the staterooms on that deck. He ducked around people stopped on the staircase, earning an 'Oi!' from a man taking a photo of his girlfriend, and skipped down onto the bottom flight of steps.

When he got to the bottom level he had to spin around 180 degrees and re-orient himself and work out which corridor she'd gone down. He sprinted into the entrance to the corridor on the port side and immediately saw Maria about fifty yards in front of him. He wanted to run but he knew she would hear his footsteps, even on this thick-pile carpet. So he walked as fast as he could without giving himself away. If she looked round now she could dive through an exit, or through a crew-only door and be gone again.

The distance between them was shrinking fast, but so was the distance between Maria and the end of the corridor. Pretty soon she would stop and let herself into her stateroom, or – if she'd heard him coming – run out the other end and disappear up or down a staircase.

Barker couldn't wait any longer. He was within 20 yards and his lack of fitness was catching up with him. He had to go now. He launched himself into a sprint as softly as he could manage and covered the distance in a few seconds. Maria heard him coming and turned her head, but couldn't escape. Barker grabbed her left arm and pushed her into the recessed doorway of the Deck Four laundry.

He'd never usually handle a woman like this, but was too fired up to care after what she'd said to him in the theatre, but Maria had another surprise for him. In the space of two seconds, she grabbed his shirt, spun him round so that his back was now up against the laundry door, pressed her right forearm across his throat, and buried her right knee firmly in his crotch.

"What the hell are you doing John?" Maria hissed in Barker's face.

"What am I doing?" Barker replied after getting some of his breath back, "Who the hell are you? What do you mean about hurting those closest to me?"

"I'm trying to help you John."

"Help me? This doesn't feel much like helping me."

"You're in over your head John. I've tried to keep my distance and hope that you wouldn't get into trouble. But now that trouble has started you're walking towards it rather than keeping out of it."

"What do you know about the trouble on this ship?"

At that moment, a stateroom door opened nearby and two people chatting loudly emerged into the corridor and

148

headed towards them. Maria relaxed her weight off Barker's throat, slipping her right hand behind his head. She stood up straighter and with her left hand around his waist pulled herself closer to him in more of an embrace than a headlock. The people passed by, smiling at the couple cuddling in the doorway and their voices faded as they turned out of the corridor towards the lifts. Maria relaxed a little and took half a step back.

"That's not important. But I know they will hurt you again if you try to stop them. You didn't need to come. He shouldn't have sent you."

"He? Who do you mean 'He'?" Barker replied puzzled, but Maria's expression changed, realising she'd said too much, and she backed away. A group of four people entered the corridor from the staircase a few yards away. Maria waited until they were close and stepped out in front of them, leaving Barker stuck in the doorway, and was gone.

Chapter 49

Barker opened the door to his stateroom and stumbled over to his bed and sat down, his head spinning. He knew he should have followed her but she was clearly able to make him regret it if she wanted to and he was exhausted and confused. What did she mean *He shouldn't have sent you?* How could she know about him and how he got here? Did she mean Rob? How could she know?

He grabbed his cell phone and searched for Rob's number and hit the dial button. Nothing. Well, why would there be a signal in the middle of the Atlantic, he thought, and turned it off. Then he remembered you could make ship-to-shore calls on the stateroom phone. It would cost a small fortune but it had to be done. He picked up his phone again and found Rob's number, adding the international dialling code, he pressed the digits into the room's phone dial. After three rings a voice said, "Hello?"

"Rob. Is that you? It's John…"

After a pause of about five seconds, Barker repeated, "Rob, it's me. John,"

Another pause then, "Hello…? Hello?"

Click. The line went dead.

Barker dialled twice more but got no answer. He put the

receiver down.

"You heard me you bastard," said Barker as he flopped back onto his bed. "What have you done?"

Chapter 50

Lucy could never go straight to sleep after a late performance so she lay in bed flicking through the movies on the on-demand TV system, hoping to find some junk that wouldn't tax her brain too much at this hour but would allow her to wind down and nod off. She remembered the Sea Star that had come through the door and looked at it on her bedside table.

She'd been watching a film for a few minutes when there was an urgent knock at the door that made her jump? She sat bolt upright and shouted, "Who is it?"

The reply was muffled so she got up and padded over to the door and looked through the spyglass to see who was in such a hurry.

"Bloody hell John, can't a girl get some sleep?" she muttered and ran back to her wardrobe drawers to find a t-shirt and some shorts.

Opening the door Lucy could see something was wrong. Barker practically pushed his way past her and sat on the end of her bed, saying, "I'm sorry, I'm sorry."

"Christ John, what's wrong?" said Lucy.

"I met Maria, in the theatre. She sat next to me. She knows who I am."

"No way? How?"

"I don't know. Or I didn't at first but I do now...I think I do."

"What do you mean?"

"She warned me to keep my nose out. She said they would hurt me if I didn't, and that 'He shouldn't have sent you'."

"He? Who's he?" said Lucy, opening the mini-bar and taking out two small brandy bottles, giving one to Barker.

"Exactly? That can only mean one person. Rob, my boss. Ex-boss."

"When did you last speak to him?"

"A few days ago. I've emailed him since and I've just tried to ring him. He picked up but didn't say anything."

Barker unscrewed the top of his brandy bottle and gulped half of it down, winced and sighed, staring into space.

"Well," said Lucy, pouring her brandy into a glass on her bedside table, "I can't make you feel a lot better after that, but we have got this," she said holding out the blank Sea Star.

"Who gave you that?" Barker asked.

"No idea. It just appeared under my door an hour or so ago. But I bet Igor was behind it. Drink up."

"We need to go now," Barker said urgently.

"No, not yet John. You need to rest. Besides, there are still a few people about. It will go quieter later. And I need some sleep. You can pull out the sofa bed and stay here if you want. I'll set an alarm for 4 am."

IX

DAY TEN: AT SEA

Chapter 51

The lights in the stateroom corridors were on all night, unlike the public rooms, which were either off or dimmed. It was eerie being out with not another soul in sight and not a sound to be heard apart from the occasional snore as they crept, barefoot, towards the nearest staircase. Lucy was hoping the curfew was just an exercise and there wouldn't actually be any security patrols. Whoever was attacking all these people was smart enough to avoid them anyway.

Barker had worked out the shortest route to the nearest of the two rooms they had numbers for: *Mitchell 10244*, up to Deck Ten and towards mid-ships. Opting to use a lift, they got there within a couple of minutes and Lucy pulled the blank Sea Star from her pocket and handed it to Barker, who swiped it quickly over the door handle, pushing it open quietly and ushering Lucy inside.

It was pitch black in the room and smelled unoccupied, but with a faint memory of perfume. Knowing how prone the heavy doors were to slamming shut, Barker eased it closed quietly before pressing a light switch so they could see what they were doing. He put his finger to his lips and looked at Lucy, who looked at him and said, 'Have you ever heard your neighbour's TV in their room?'

"No," said Barker quietly.

"That's because they're soundproof John." Lucy replied.

"I just don't want to arouse suspicion."

"We won't, just talk quietly and don't knock anything over."

The double bed had been made, and clothes were hanging in the wardrobe. There were shoes on the floor by the side of the bed, lined up as though the stateroom steward had sorted them. Barker noticed there were three types: a man's, and woman's and some smaller trainers, probably belonging to a young boy. Lucy nodded and pointed to the ceiling where two drop-down bunks were stored. "Family room," she said. "This must be the traffic accident. I heard it was a family involved."

"Why is their stuff still here?" asked Barker.

Lucy shrugged, "Well I guess they would've gone straight to the hospital, but the ship would have to leave regardless. It looks like it's been tidied. I think the staff will pack it all up when the cruise ends and ship it to them. The cases are probably under the bed."

Barker pushed back the valance on the front of the bed and sure enough, there were three cases squeezed underneath.

"Will their passports be here?" asked Barker

"They'll be in the safe if they are, but someone might have collected them on the day, for the police," said Lucy.

In the corner diagonally opposite the door, near to the balcony door, there was a dressing table, with makeup and perfume bottles and a hairdryer laid out, plus a few random bits and bobs: plug adaptor, sun cream, a pen, some jewellery. Nothing that could give them much information.

Lucy came out of the bathroom having had a look around and shook her head at Barker. "Nothing," she said, "What's that?" pointing to a loose pile of paperwork on a small table opposite the dresser.

Barker turned and picked up the pile and spread it out on the bed.

"Travel documents," he said, "Cruise itinerary, excursions, Gibraltar factsheet, tickets, daily newsletters."

Lucy took a few of the papers as Barker put them on the bed, putting them back into a pile once she'd dismissed them. One of the tickets caused her to stop and look twice. It was about 6 inches by 3 inches and didn't look the same as the ship's stationery.

"They won the cruise," Lucy said, raising her eyebrows. "In a competition. Poor sods."

Barker took the ticket and had a look himself, then he folded it in half and put it in his back pocket.

"Come on," he said, "Gibson, 13118."

Chapter 52

It was further to the next stateroom. They walked quietly along the corridor towards the forward staircase and crept carefully up three decks, watching around every corner. It seemed like Lucy was right and there was no one around. The silence was deafening. It was normally quiet at night, but you would usually hear a lift or a cleaner or some late-night revellers making their way to bed. There would almost certainly be some activity on the Lido Deck but they didn't have to go that far up.

On Deck Thirteen they headed back down the corridor a short way to room 13118. Barker took the Sea Star again and let them into the room, turning the light on once the door was closed.

This room was a mirror image of the previous one. Everything was the opposite way around, but the layout was otherwise identical. The bed had been made but the room was much tidier. Bottles on the dresser showed it had been occupied by a woman, and the dresses in the wardrobe showed it was an older woman on her own.

A pile of papers similar to the one in 10244 was on a bedside table, stacked more neatly. Barker flicked through but nothing caught his eye. Lucy checked the bathroom again but saw nothing interesting. But this time she noticed a handbag sat on the floor of the wardrobe. She picked it up and took it to the bed and began to go through the contents. Lipstick, powder compact, earrings, small perfume bottle, tissues, pen, stamps. Then she unzipped a side pocket and slipped her hand inside, to find a few bits of paper and card. Some phone numbers and addresses, and a ticket the same as they'd found in the other room.

Lucy looked up and passed the ticket to Barker, who read it, looked at Lucy, and slipped it into his pocket with the other one.

Chapter 53

Upstairs in a three-bedroomed semi-detached red brick house on a quiet, leafy residential street in Surrey, just after midnight, Katie Mitchell gently closed the door to her son Josh's bedroom, leaving on his bedside lamp. It was the second time that night he'd woken up crying and gone to find her. She'd spent the last hour sitting on his bed talking about his Dad. Why *him*, Josh wanted to know? And would the same person come for his Mum too? Katie found it impossible to explain it all to him because she didn't have the answers.

It was almost a week since Jack had died in hospital in Gibraltar, from serious head wounds inflicted by the hit-and-run driver that narrowly missed her and Josh but fatally wounded her husband. The police were treating it as a traffic accident and had found the burnt-out wreck of the car less than a mile away. But her gut instinct told Katie there was more to it, and not just because of her grief. It happened so fast. It just seemed so deliberate. And what about the woman on the scooter? Did *she* see anything?

Chapter 54

Back in room 3163 Lucy switched on the kettle and turned over the two mugs that Clifford had placed there in the early evening when he tidied the room.

"Hot chocolate?" she said.

"What? Now? Erm, yeah OK." Barker replied.

Lucy ripped open two sachets and poured them into the cups and went to sit on the end of her bed next to Barker.

"Come on, let's see 'em," she said.

Barker slipped his hand in his back pocket and pulled out the two folded tickets, flattened them out, and put them on the bed between them. They picked up one each. The cards were thick and textured and a mottled pale pink in colour. Printed on them were some decorative flourishes around the edges and corners and text in two different, badly-matched fonts.

"'Savenas Seaways relaunch promotion cruise competition proudly congratulates Mrs M Gibson'," Lucy began, "'You are the winner of our once in a lifetime Caribbean cruise giveaway', blah blah dates, blah Claim Your Voucher Here, website address, terms & conditions apply. Doesn't tell us much."

Barker looked back down at his ticket, "'Savenas Seaways relaunch promotion cruise competition proudly congratulates

Mr S Mitchell. You are the winner of our once in a lifetime Caribbean cruise giveaway', Yep. Same."

"Odd," said Lucy.

"What is?" Barker replied.

"'You are *the* winner.' On both tickets. Not *a* winner, *the* winner. I thought you said you were a policeman," Lucy said, grinning at Barker.

"Retired."

"By six months!"

"Whatever," said Barker, reluctantly returning the grin, "Yes it is a bit odd. But if a killer wanted to get a group of people onto a cruise he or she wouldn't want them to know about each other – not until they got here at least."

"...and we're back in the room."

"Watch it."

"I'll take one of these to Igor first thing and see if he recognises them, just to make sure we're not going down a blind alley."

"No, I'll take them," said Barker, "You're too noticeable."

"I'm not sure how to take that."

"You know what I mean. He knows he can trust me now and the other guests won't notice me. And I'll go at lunchtime when it's busy. You're the glamorous artiste known to passengers and crew alike. It's part of your job to be remembered. I'm Mr Anonymous."

"Thanks John...I think. And don't put yourself down. You're average at least."

Lucy couldn't help herself from giggling but shook her head and looked down at the ticket again. "A handful of people have been killed on this ship in a week and here I am laughing."

"Nervous tension?" Barker suggested.

"Lack of sleep," said Lucy standing up and walking over to the boiling kettle to fill up the cups.

"So, anyone else with one of these tickets is in danger?"

"You were doing so well John, I could've worked that one out for myself. Here, drink this. It'll help you sleep. Give your brain some rest."

"Sleep? It's nearly time to get up."

"Yes and my first show is at 11.30 am and I've had about three hours so far. I need another three at least. Drink that and we'll go to bed. There's a sofa bed..." Lucy quickly added, gulping her hot chocolate and pointing across the room. It was the first time Barker had seen her blush.

"I'll go back to my own room," Barker suggested.

"No. No, you won't. Stay here. We've had a successful night. I was crapping myself when we were sneaking around before, dreading getting caught. I could maybe have come up with a cover story for myself, but you'd have been in big trouble. Drink up and I'll turn the light out. If you want to leave when the curfew ends at seven that's fine but don't you dare wake me up!"

"Meet me for lunch in the Atrium at one O'Clock?"

"If I'm awake, yes."

Chapter 55

Marcus Jackson liked to be up early and outside not long after the sun came up. He didn't like crowds and there were specific areas of the Lido Deck where he could and couldn't sit, even given the choice of almost all of the sun loungers and tables at this time of day. Some were too noisy, some too hot, some too windy. If he didn't get up early enough and find his spot it would ruin his day. He wasn't a people person, whatever that meant. He'd been told that more than once, including by his employer. He couldn't actually understand why he needed to be. He worked in a cubicle at a computer all day, moving information from his head to his hard drive. He wasn't a salesman. They might need to be people-oriented. He wasn't like his older brother, Mr Popular, who got promoted every six months because of all the hand-shaking and back-scratching he did. He sometimes wondered why that's why he turned out the way he was. After all, siblings tend to not want to be like the other one sometimes, don't they? Mr Popular, or Matt as everyone else preferred to call him, was always the favourite. Their parents made no secret of that. Matt this, Matt that. Why can't you be more like Matt?

Eventually, Marcus found himself in one of his preferred corners and sat at a table on the end of the row and furthest from the noisy Skyscape restaurant. He was outside for the fresh air but not near the pool for the screaming and the sunburn. It wasn't exactly quiet but he could make a quick exit if it got too much for him. Otherwise he would sit here for exactly three hours reading his book and working on his laptop, until it was time to go for his breakfast after the hordes had eaten theirs and the restaurant was relatively sane again before lunch kicked in. He had paid extra for the full internet package that meant he could access all his usual online haunts if he needed to feel connected, but he recognised the need to 'be on holiday' as his parents had told him repeatedly.

After breakfast he would go inside, avoiding the peak noise, peak heat and peak people period that everyone else seemed to love. He would also look more out of place at that time anyway. He was aware of his odd appearance. He hadn't packed a single pair of shorts and had no intention of going in the pool. So he sat gently sweating in his comfy baggy jeans and t-shirt, while everyone else was stripping off down to shorts and stringy bikinis with bits of their bodies hanging out that should be covered up instead of distracting him. More than most people, he fought the urge to glance at the beautiful bodies that wandered past now and then. He'd had far too many death-stares from young women that had caught him sneaking a look. On the odd occasion one would show a hint of a smile he would just wonder what was wrong with them. Or him. He was happy being on his own. Or at least used to the idea by now.

Chapter 56

In the queue at the grandly-named Guest Relations desk, a short walk from the forward end of the Atrium's lower floor on Deck Five, Barker was feeling the effects of very little sleep but trying to stay alert in case he was noticed. By whom he wasn't sure, other than Maria, who he was dreading bumping into again, but he figured she would keep a low profile for now. Nobody else would notice just another guest making a complaint at the reception desk.

As he edged forwards he tried to work out how he was going to make sure he got to see Igor and not one of the other three people at the desk. With one person in front of him in the queue he thought he had timed it right. A staff member became available and the lady in front walked over to her. Igor was smiling sweetly at his customer and she turned away, walked a few paces, then spun around and went back to him, just as another assistant became free. Barker turned around and said to the elderly man behind him, 'You go next. I need to speak to the man on the end.'

Igor's customer eventually finished her second enquiry and walked away satisfied, but Igor's smile dropped a little when he saw his next job was to speak to Barker.

"Good afternoon sir, how can I help you?" Igor said, raising a nervous smile.

"Hello," John replied, trying to remain formal, as if they'd not met before, "I found this ticket on the floor last night and wondered if you could tell me if it was an official Galaxy Cruises competition?" He locked eyes with Igor as he said the last four words.

Igor took the ticket and looked at it for a few seconds and locked eyes with Barker again, "No Sir, definitely not. We have no competition winners from Galaxy, but it could be from an agent. Do you need it?"

Slightly surprised at the thought of handing over the ticket, Barker remembered the other, almost identical one, and figured he didn't. "No. No, thank you."

"I will shred it for you then sir," said Igor nervously. "Good afternoon."

"Yes, please do," replied Barker checking Igor's expression as he turned away.

Igor took the ticket and dropped it into a cardboard box underneath the desk with all the day's other items for shredding. Barker messaged Lucy asking to meet in the Atrium mid-afternoon when it would be quietest.

Chapter 57

Lucy knew she'd find Barker in the coffee shop on Deck Five, the lowest floor of the Atrium. He had ordered a sandwich but she couldn't eat too soon after her first performance of the day, so just ordered a strong coffee.

"How can we find out if there are others in danger?" Barker asked Lucy.

"You're the policeman." She replied.

"I know. I'm thinking out loud."

"OK. I couldn't tell the difference."

"I mean how can we see if anyone else on the ship has one of these tickets?"

"You really think that's the key?"

"It's all we have, isn't it? It's the only link we have between two of the victims. It's a start."

"Suppose so. So we have to get a message out that's not too obvious?" Lucy paused for a moment, and added, 'There's always Stardate."

"The newsletter? We can't broadcast it." John replied, confused.

"No, but we need to reach everybody quickly and that's the only way to do it. Everyone gets one in their room every evening and scans through it. It's a bit of an event. They tried to get rid of it when the phone app was launched, but the passengers complained. They like it. Costs a fortune to print fifteen hundred copies every day."

"So what do we say? How can we ask people in a public newsletter?"

"I can tell you're new to cruising. Have you noticed a meeting called 'Friends of Bill W' in it most days?"

"Can't say I have. Who's Bill W?"

"Doesn't matter. That's Alcoholics Anonymous."

"What?" said Barker, taken aback.

"AA. There are bars everywhere on a cruise ship. It would be so easy to relapse. So they have meetings every day for people with drink problems. And there's 'Friends of Dorothy' too."

"Go on."

"Actually, most cruises just list it as what it is now, LGBTQ or something like that."

"So how does that help us?" asked Barker, "We can't advertise for suspected murder targets."

"Use your imagination John."

Lucy picked up the remaining ticket from her bedside table and read it out loud.

"'Savenas Seaways relaunch promotion cruise competition proudly congratulates Mrs M Gibson. You are the winner of our once-in-a-lifetime Caribbean cruise giveaway. Claim Your Voucher Here.' So we put in a meeting for 'Friends of Savenas Seaways,'" Lucy said, looking up at Barker.

"As simple as that?" Barker responded.

Lucy's optimistic face frowned, "Yes. As simple as that."

"What if the killer sees it?"

"Well...Well then we're screwed," Lucy said, deflated. "No! Actually, it doesn't make any difference, does it? He'll already

171

know where they all are anyway so this won't make any difference."

"It will tip him off that we know about Savenas."

Lucy paused in thought. "Not necessarily. It could mean that some ticket 'winners' have met each other and arranged a get-together. It doesn't mean they realise what's going on yet. *We're* going to tell them that."

"How do we do it?" said Barker, a little more positively.

"Submit it to the events team. I'll fill a form in and say it was suggested to me by a guest who was too shy to ask herself. I know the team and I know a girl in the office. They arrange my schedule for me so they won't think too much of it."

"And that'll get out tonight?"

"Yes."

"OK, do it. We don't have much time and I can't think of any better options."

Chapter 58

Whoever approved the title of Starlight's daily newsletter, Stardate, may or may not have been aware of the word's Sci-Fi origin. No doubt most of the passengers weren't, but they did like receiving it as part of their on-board routine, even after it was effectively replaced by Galaxy's own app which passengers used to check-in, order drinks on deck, locate one another around the ship, and check the daily schedule of events in real-time, all on their own cell phones.

Stardate was just a traditional four-page A4 folded leaflet delivered to each stateroom every evening by the cabin stewards when they came to turn down your bed while the guests were having dinner. It had a colourful, glossy layout packed with information and a few photographs. The back page was always standard ship information; safety advice, locations of services and contact numbers. The front picked out a few of the highlights from the following day's scheduled events and usually had a message from a member of the crew, as well as a reminder of that day's dress code in the dining room, plus what time the ship was scheduled to be arriving in port, if at all. Passengers could often be seen carrying their copies around the ship, reading them in bars and lounges, checking out the inside pages for all the detailed information about every event happening on the ship from early morning yoga classes, to table tennis competitions on deck, films being shown on the Lido Deck, to the times of the shows being performed in the theatre.

Squeezed into Stardate: 13.09.19 DAY9, in the morning section, was a line saying,

9.30am – Adriatic Suite – Friends of Savenas

X

DAY ELEVEN: AT SEA

Chapter 59

Just before 9 am the next morning, Lucy came out of a crew-only doorway on Deck Five at the forward end of the ship near to the lowest floor of the theatre, and next to the entrance to the Spa on the starboard side. A lobby connected across to the port side and in the middle was the entrance to a conference room called the Adriatic Suite. Lucy was wearing jeans and a t-shirt with her hair scraped back as much as possible under a baseball cap, and wearing a pair of glasses that she normally never wore outside of her room, in an effort to be as invisible as possible. Over her shoulder, she carried a small rucksack.

The door to the suite was closed as expected and nobody else was outside, so she turned around and walked up to it and put her ear up against it. Remembering that most ship doors are heavy and soundproof, she pushed the handle down and opened the door gently, ready to apologise to anyone that might already be inside. But the bland, corporate-style room where the captain occasionally performed wedding ceremonies was empty apart from a couple of dozen chairs in two blocks and a desk at the front about thirty feet away under a whiteboard, and a projector on the ceiling. So far, so boring. Perfect.

She went inside and pushed the door almost closed, leaving

it open an inch to indicate to Barker that she was inside. Two minutes later, he followed her quietly into the room. A minute after that, Lucy peeked her head out and stuck a laminated A4 sign on the outside of the door, on Galaxy Cruises headed paper, simply saying 'Friends of Savenas'.

"Who's doing the talking?" asked Barker.

"Hadn't thought," replied Lucy.

"I think you should start. You're friendlier, more of a people-person."

"Oh, OK. If you like."

"What do we..." Lucy began before her heart bounced as the door was pushed open and in walked a small, dark-haired middle-aged woman who looked like she never normally saw the sun, but had overdone the last few days on deck.

"What's this all about then?" she said, "'Friends of Save-nas'? Does this include me?"

"Good morning Mrs...?" Lucy began, walking over to the woman and offering her hand.

"Merrifield. Janet Merrifield." Replied the woman, relaxing a little but looking suspiciously at Barker who just smiled awkwardly and stuck out a hand to usher her into the room.

Lucy guided Mrs Merrifield up to the far end of the room while frantically working out her opening speech. "Hello Janet. Yes, come in, sit down up here. That's what we're here to explain," said Lucy, showing Janet to a seat on the front row nearest to the desk and putting her rucksack on it and pulling out a clipboard and pens. Lucy looked up at Barker who returned her glance with an approving smile.

"It seems there's more than one prize winner and we've had a few questions. Would you mind just putting your name down on this sheet so we remember who attended?" Lucy handed

Janet the clipboard and a Galaxy Cruises pen stolen from the front desk.

"There's no problem with the cruise competition is there? There are so many horrible things happening on here, nothing would surprise me."

"No, no, you're perfectly fine. Have you enjoyed it so far? I mean, apart from the...disruption?"

"Well, yes, obviously. A free cruise: can't complain. And we didn't even have to do anything. All we did was fill in the coupon and send our name and address in, and here we are. Doesn't happen every day that does it?"

"No," said Lucy, "No, it doesn't Janet. What's your husband's name by the way? You are here with your husband aren't you?"

"Yes, yes I am. Shall I put his name down too?"

"Yes please," said Lucy, pleased with her forward-thinking, "we might need his details as well."

Barker was impressed with Lucy's improvisation and left her to it and loitered about near the door, keeping half an eye open for other attendees. A handful of people had walked by and a couple were standing around in the lobby outside.

"What are we here for? Who else is coming?" said Janet, adding her husband Malcolm's name to the sheet.

"Well, Janet, it's a bit strange. It seems that there's more than one winner of the competition, and we wanted to find all of you so we get the full picture. It was an unofficial competition you see, and there's been a few problems contacting Savenas about it. But it has no effect on your cruise. We just want to get as much information as possible."

"How many winners are there?" Janet asked.

"We don't know yet," said Lucy, "That's what today is for.

To see who's involved and that you're all getting the service you were promised. Galaxy wants to make sure you're all happy and safe. Have you bumped into anyone you know so far?"

"No, should I have done?" replied Janet. "Oh, I did see a young man a couple of times who I thought I recognised. Couldn't place him I'm afraid. On his own, I think. A bit strange looking."

"Oh well, never mind. It's amazing how often you bump into familiar faces on holiday isn't it?" said Lucy, looking at Barker and wondering how long she could keep this up.

Barker shrugged back at her just as the door creaked open again and a couple walked in and looked at him as curiously as Janet Merrifield had done a few minutes earlier. They were younger, in their early thirties, but equally puzzled.

"Good morning. We wondered what this 'Friends of Save-nas' was about. Is it to do with the competition?"

"Yes, yes it is. Good morning. Lucy over there will explain and take your details," said Barker, ushering them forward into the room.

Sam and Jordan Smithson walked over to Lucy, shook hands, took a seat, and listened to much the same as Janet had before them. Lucy was stretching the introductions out as much as she could in the hope that more people would arrive, but with no idea how many to expect she eventually ran out of ideas and was about to try to hand over to Barker, when a slightly scruffy younger man in shorts and t-shirt walked through the door, closely followed by a petite young Asian woman around the same age. Barker assumed they were a couple, but they both politely denied it when they were introduced to Lucy and asked to sign the sheet on the clipboard. Janet looked pointedly at

Lucy and mouthed the words, "That's him," while tipping her head slightly in the direction of the new arrival, as if Lucy was supposed to learn something from it. The young woman smiled and waved timidly at Janet, who frowned at first and then beamed. "Oh hello Jasmine! We were just talking about bumping into people we knew weren't we?" she said, glancing at Lucy, "And I said I hadn't so far. How are you?"

"That's probably everyone now," said Barker, shutting the door a little too firmly, and walked up to the front of the room.

"Probably, yes," said Lucy, "Do you want to take over for me John?" she said, looking at Barker hopefully. He recognised that as an instruction rather than a request and took over.

"Oh OK. Thank you for coming to see us, everyone. We had no idea how many would turn up..."

"What's the problem?" interrupted the young man who had sat on his own in the second row of seats.

"Problem? I'm sorry, what's your name?" replied Barker.

"Marcus. Yeah, what's the problem? There's no drinks, no food. This isn't supposed to be fun is it? So there must be a problem."

Slightly thrown by Marcus's attitude, Barker continued, "Thanks Marcus. Well, yes and no. There's no problem with your cruise, but the competition you entered, well we think it was fraudulent."

A few eyebrows were raised as the visitors began muttering to each other.

"Do any of you know or have any connection to Savenas?"

Silent shaking of heads and looking around at each other.

"Galaxy have no knowledge of this competition," Barker continued, raising his voice a little, "Except that your tickets were paid for independently by several different entities in different parts of the world. You're as entitled to be here as anyone else, so don't worry about that. Do you all have a ticket like this?" Barker held up one of the tickets he and Lucy had taken from the staterooms.

Everyone except Marcus nodded. "My Mum and Dad got one but gave it to me when it arrived. They get seasick. So why do we need to know this if everything's OK?"

Barker breathed in deeply. "I'm an officer from the Metropolitan Police in London. We think you might be in danger. We think the person that gave you your tickets could be responsible for some of the incidents that have happened on the ship this week."

The stunned silence that followed seemed to last for minutes as Janet's mouth fell open, and everyone stared at Barker, including Lucy, who was almost as stunned, more at Barker's decisiveness than what he actually said. She hadn't expected him to come straight out with it.

"Bullshit!" shouted Marcus, "Why would you say that?"

"Because, Marcus..." Barker began, "Look, I'm sorry. I didn't mean to startle you all but it's important you know, for your own safety. There have been several deaths on the ship since we left – more than you might be aware of – and at least two of them also had these tickets."

"Two?! That's called a coincidence."

"We're going to find the others, I'm sure. And if we don't..."

"What a waste of time," said Marcus as he stood up and walked to the door.

"Marcus, stop, please," Barker pleaded, "stay in your room. Everyone should stay in their rooms for a couple of days until we know more. Sit on your balcony, use room service, watch a mov..."

"I don't have a balcony. I traded it for an inside stateroom. I don't like the sun," said Marcus as he opened the door and left.

Keen to avoid any more early departures, Lucy decided to step in and soften the blow a little.

"We really hope we're wrong, but we just want to be absolutely sure that there's no risk to you at all. John's right. You should stay in your rooms until we know more. I know it's a lot to ask and you don't know us but..."

"'You're the singer." Jasmine interrupted, "From the bar, from the Atrium. Why are you telling us this? Why isn't someone from the staff here?"

"Well I...John and I...We..."

"I asked Lucy to help me," Barker interrupted, saving Lucy's blushes, "I needed someone who knew the ship, how things work and what normally happens on board. But I can't ask the crew. They wouldn't tell me anything, their job is to keep everyone calm and sort it out later."

"But why not let them?" said Jordan, sat right in front of Barker.

Barker hesitated before adding, "Because I think I might be involved too. I think they might have attacked my wife."

More silence.

"Look I hope we're wrong, but give us twenty-four hours to find out something else. If we don't come up with anything I'll buy you all dinner in one of the speciality restaurants – your choice."

Chapter 60

In Funchal, Rebecca Collins had been summoned to the hospital to sign for the release of her husband David's body. His mother Diane had wanted to be there but delays meant they'd had to get a return flight the previous day and couldn't wait any longer.

Rebecca walked down the sterile hospital corridors in a daze and found the office where she'd been told to report to and ask for Dr Mendes. She waited ten minutes before being ushered into a small room with just a few chairs and a low table, like the one she'd been in on the day she arrived when the doctor told her how she thought David had died.

Dr Christina Mendes walked in a few seconds later, closed the door behind her and gently smiled at Rebecca.

"Good afternoon Rebecca. We have the coroner's report and it does confirm that David died of natural causes," said the doctor quietly.

After a deep breath, Rebecca replied. "But he was so fit. We had no idea he had any health problems, certainly none that could kill him."

"I know. It's such a shock when it happens like this, I'm so sorry. It not as uncommon as we would like to think, I'm afraid."

"There was nothing suspicious? Nothing that seemed strange?"

"No. Our tests found nothing. We've been very thorough. It does mean that we can release his body for transportation home. Will your insurance company take care of that?"

"Yes," Rebecca nodded, staring out in front of her, "we always bought good insurance. Never expected to need it."

Chapter 61

"So did we achieve anything?" Lucy said to Barker as they sat on the Starboard side of the ship at a table by the window in the Skyscape restaurant during the brief lull between breakfast and lunch. Both nursed a mug of over-brewed coffee.

"I'm not sure," Barker replied, turning his gaze back to her after staring out to sea for several minutes.

"We got a few names, and we know more tickets exist," Lucy said positively.

"We're no further on though. Where does that leave us?"

"You're the policeman. You tell me."

"We need to tackle Maria again. She's the only person we know is involved somehow."

"That's not gone well so far."

Barker looked up at Lucy with a blank expression.

"Sorry," said Lucy.

"It's OK, I'm just thinking back to what she said. 'They will hurt the ones closest to you. You of all people should know that', 'They will hurt you again' and what she said about Rob."

"For what it's worth I think we should come at it from a different angle."

"How do you mean?"

"Well, we don't know who Savenas Seaways is do we?

There's got to be a clue there."

"Probably just a made-up name."

"Maybe, but it's got to be worth trying to find out who's behind it. That's going to give us more than Maria Cortez."

"Maybe you're right. I'll go and do some digging, see what I can find."

"I'll speak to Igor again. See if he can give us anything else. He'll do anything for a few Pina Coladas."

Chapter 62

Sir Lynden Oscar Pindling is regarded as the Father of the Nation of the Bahamas, having led it to independence in July 1973 and served as its Prime Minister from 1969 to 1992. The International airport named after him was having a busy day as the season began to ramp up to its usual Christmas peak, when tourists from Europe would arrive for some winter sun. Two pale-faced people, one male one female, walked side by side wheeling carry-on cases from their arrival gate into the immigration area and looked vacantly around. They didn't look as happy to be there as most of the other foreigners arriving that day. They had travelled together but were not a couple. And they hadn't come for a holiday.

Paul Sanderson's older sister Samantha had won a competition that sent her on the holiday she'd always dreamed of, a Caribbean cruise, only for it to turn into her worst nightmare. Charlotte Hamilton was the twin sister of Samantha's husband, Jonathan Howard. The couple's parents had to stay at home to look after their now orphaned children, while Paul and Charlotte volunteered to travel to identify their bodies.

The airline had taken pity on them and given them first-class accommodation on board so they had both got some sleep on the nine-hour flight from Heathrow. But neither of them looked fresh when they arrived, still shell-shocked, in the capital of the Bahamas, Nassau.

After shuffling in the immigration queue for ten minutes, Charlotte stepped up to the desk just before Paul. The man behind it took a long look at her and waved to an official at the side of the room, who squeezed the button on the side of the radio attached to his jacket and spoke into it.

"Is this Mr Sanderson?" the man behind the desk said, gesturing at Paul to come forward.

"Yes. Yes it is," said Charlotte weakly, turning to look behind her.

"Please, go to that gentleman over there. He will take you to the security office."

The man with the radio was already on his way over and gestured to Charlotte and Paul, who easily fell into step behind him as he led them out through a side door.

Chapter 63

Around midday Barker stepped out of a glass elevator on Deck Six, turned right, and walked around the Atrium and into the iCafe for the second time. He knew how old-fashioned an internet cafe was these days, but there were a lot of older people on board and the ship's WiFi was so expensive. It was probably better to pay for it in small chunks so you knew how much debt you were racking up.

He had no idea how much he could find out about Savenas Seaways using just a search engine and a lot of luck, but it was the most obvious thing to do first. He logged in using Lucy's password again, waited a few seconds for it to connect and typed Savenas Seaways into the empty search box. A list of random websites and products and blogs with Savenas Seaways in their name came up and his heart sank for a second. This could take forever. He typed 'Savenas Seaways company' to try to narrow it down. A more focussed but still long list appeared and he realised he didn't know which country Savenas Seaways would be based in, if any. But he figured it would be good to start with British or American business so looked for the filter to reduce the results further.

Barker sifted through the likely entries one by one, checking if anything about them rang any bells. He became so engrossed in the search he didn't notice the tall, thin older man sit down at a PC in the row behind him until he spoke.

"I thought you'd know who they are."

Barker, slightly startled, sat up from his hunched position and turned around on his swivel chair to face the man. "I'm sorry?"

"I thought you'd know who Savenas Seaways are. You know, since you organised a meeting about them."

The man looked directly at Barker accusingly.

"I don't recognise you from the meeting," Barker replied guardedly.

"That's because I wasn't there," said the man.

"I'm not following."

"Well, I was there, but not at the meeting."

"You're going to have to explain..."

"I was hanging around outside. I waited for the meeting to end to see who would come out. I recognised some of the people who attended, but not you or your friend. So how come you don't know who they are?"

Barker was getting frustrated with the man and turned back to his PC saying, "You should've come to the meeting."

"Perhaps. But it turned out I didn't need to once I saw who was there. I know who Savenas Seaways are and I think I can help you. My name's Eric Spencer."

Barker turned his chair around again and looked the man up and down.

"The man from the Atrium?"

"You've done your homework."

"You're looking well."

"Thank you. I was lucky. I'm a fairly fit man and he was a bad shot."

Barker looked around to make sure there was nobody listening.

"So who are Savenas Seaways and why are you willing to help?"

"Well, I'm helping because somebody shot at me, and I think that person was hired by a company called ABJ Transatlantic who are a client of mine."

"A client? Who are ABJ Transatlantic?"

"I'm an accountant. I retrained after leaving the Navy. I had contacts in the merchant navy so I found work with shipping and cargo companies like ABJ."

"So what does that have to do with Savenas Seaways?"

"Savenas is an anagram of Vanessa, The MD of ABJ puts money into a subsidiary company of that name when he wants to hide it, or when he's being less than honest about where it's come from. Vanessa is the name of his dead wife. Very few people would know that. When I saw 'Friends of Savenas' in Stardate I was curious, bearing in mind what's been going on."

"Why would you suspect them of anything like this?"

"Well, Mr...?"

Barker hesitated, should he give his real name or a fake name? He went with real name. "Barker."

"Well, Mr Barker, ABJ is a major shareholder in Galaxy Cruises. I might be wrong, but something just doesn't smell right."

"You think they'd go as far as trying to get rid of you?"

"Unlikely but not impossible. They might make it known how useful it would be if I met with an accident. Word spreads to the wrong sort of people, favours are owed. One thing leads to another..."

"And you end up with a bullet wound?"

"Just a graze really. I had worse when I was on active service, but I'm older now."

Barker's phone pinged with a text message alert, from Lucy.

Igor has room info. Got a date with him at nine. Can fit you in for dinner at seven ;)

Pick you up at ten-to. You can tell me all about Savenas Seaways.

"Good timing," Barker muttered to himself. For a couple of seconds he wondered what he was supposed to do with the information from Igor, then he remembered he still had the master Sea Star and Lucy would know that.

"Urgent?" said Eric Spencer.

"No," replied Barker, "Important but not urgent. Tell me more."

Chapter 64

When Lucy arrived in Skywalker's nightclub just after nine, Igor was sat on a stool by the bar talking to the bartender and a group of women who probably knew him from his work on the Guest Relations desk. He wasn't the sort of person who could blend into the background. Lucy had deliberately been late so she wouldn't have to hang around for him, knowing that he was always early and never alone for very long.

"There you are Lucy babe!" said Igor excitedly as he introduced his new friends to her and ushered her onto the stool next to him. The three women said hello and made their excuses and left them to talk, although talking wasn't easy over the bouncing of the music and shouting of the guests. "What are you drinking?"

"Mojito," replied Lucy "you should know that!" she said, shouting over the noise. "Good day?"

"Ah, usual," said Igor, "Dealing with complaints, telling people where things are after nearly two weeks on board, calming people who are worrying about trouble on ship. But I smile, I always smile. Don't let it make me miserable. How about you?"

"Yeah, did a couple of sets this afternoon and I'm on again at eleven in the Explorers lounge. Late finish for me. I'll be knackered tomorrow."

"And your boyfriend?"

"Igor!"

"Oh come on. You two always together. I see you walking to dining room earlier. Not a problem if you like older man. Like I do." Igor beamed at Lucy and sipped his drink through his straw.

"Well, as you brought it up, you said you had some info for me. For John anyway."

Igor put his drink on the bar and steadied himself with his right hand and fished his phone out of his pocket, tapping at the image gallery and showing the screen to Lucy. It was a photograph of part of an email sent to the housekeeping department asking them to clean room 11376 Howard. Lucy took her phone out of her tiny handbag and sent Barker a message repeating the basics.

Howard, 11376. Good luck.

"Right, business over," Lucy said, putting her drink down and grabbing Igor by the hand, "We're here to dance. Come on."

Igor slid off his stool and followed Lucy to the opposite end of the room onto the sparkling dance floor.

Chapter 65

Barker's phone pinged again, as he sat in the Piano Lounge near the Atrium nursing a glass of craft beer while pretending to be interested in the music and watching people drift in looking for seats after dinner and before going to see the show in the theatre. Another message from Lucy. A name and a number.

"That was quick," he thought. He'd only left her twenty minutes ago after dinner in the Four Seasons restaurant. Lucy had surprised him this time with a quiet table for two in a corner where they could 'talk business' but it was hard for him not to imagine it was more than that. He enjoyed her company and while they were involved in this... whatever it was, he could pretend it would go on forever. But they were nearing the final port and in a few days would he ever see her again? She would carry on singing on cruise ships and he would head back to Spain to continue rebuilding his lonely life. He wondered whether he cared about solving crimes any more but shook himself out of his melancholy and re-read the name and number she'd sent him.

Howard, 11376. Good luck.

"Part-timer," he said to himself as he swigged the last of his beer, stood up, and patted the Sea Star in his trouser pocket just to make sure it was still there.

The timing was good since the cabin stewards would have been into everyone's room to turn down their beds, so wouldn't be around to wonder who the stranger was letting himself into room 11736.

Chapter 66

Lucy climbed up on the barstool and picked up her drink from where she'd left it ten minutes before. Igor followed her from the dance floor and did the same.

"The DJ is rubbish," Igor announced, "I can't dance to this."

"I agree," replied Lucy between sips of Mojito, "Never mind. He'll play something better in a few minutes. Let's sit down over there."

Lucy led Igor a few metres across the room to a booth next to a bank of windows overlooking the bow of the ship. They couldn't see out as the sun had long gone down and the blackness gave no clue as to where they were or where they might be heading.

"Pee break," Igor said as he put his drink down on the table in front of Lucy without sitting down, "Back in five."

"Oh, OK," said Lucy, suddenly left on her own as Igor turned and walked towards the entrance lobby where the bathrooms were. She picked up his drink, stood up and carried it back to the bar, and sat back on the stool again, "At least I can talk to the staff here," she said as she smiled at Yulia from Ukraine who was drying glasses and tidying the counter-top.

Ten minutes passed before the conversation with Yulia, interspersed with serving drinks to customers, had to come to an end while she went to stock up on spirits. Lucy suddenly remembered she'd moved from where Igor thought she'd be sat, and she span around and scanned the seats and the busy, noisy room. He might have been dragged to the dance floor by those friendly guests as he came back in, but she couldn't see the top of his head, which was normally the best way to spot his skinny six-foot frame in a crowd. She waited a few more minutes before messaging him:

Having trouble?

Igor's phone was always glued to his palm, unless he was working, or dancing, and even then it was in his back pocket. So Lucy's nerves started jangling a little when he hadn't replied five minutes later. She got up and wandered out into the lobby by the bathroom entrances. No sign of Igor talking to passengers, so she walked back to the bar to look for help.

"Yulia!" she shouted after waiting a few seconds for her to finish serving a customer, "is Martin working tonight?"

"Yes, he's over there waiting tables," Yulia replied point in the general direction of the dance floor.

"Thank you,"

Lucy waited until Martin had taken a couple of orders and made his way back in her direction before stopping him.

"Martin I need a favour."

"Sure Lucy, what is it?"

"I came in with Igor and he went to the bathroom about fifteen, twenty minutes ago and hasn't come back. It's not like him. And he's not answering my messages. Would you go take a look for me?"

"Sure. His battery must've died. He always has his phone. I'll pass these orders to Yulia and go take a look."

Two minutes later Martin walked back and shook his head at Lucy, "No sign of him."

XI

DAY TWELVE: AT SEA

Chapter 67

Just after 4.45 am, a tall, muscular man with short dark-brown hair, wearing an all-white officer's uniform, walked confidently through a door from Deck Sixteen and round the corner to the forward staircase and made his way down thirteen decks. He chose not to use the elevators because that might mean waiting a short while even at this time of night, there would be a polite 'ping' as the lift arrived, and he might possibly be engaged in conversation by a drunk or an insomniac. Walking was much quieter and more anonymous. People would simply nod admiringly at the officer doing his duties or clocking off for the night, and then immediately forget him.

Once he got down to Deck Three he turned out of the staircase and to his right, onto the port side of the ship, then turned left and slowed down to check the room numbers. He found the one he wanted, looked around, put his wrist up to the door handle, and pushed it down very slowly when the LED on it flashed.

Inside, the room was pitch black and warm. He closed the door as quietly as possible without it making a click and stood behind it in the darkness waiting for his eyes to adjust to what little light there was coming in under the door and from the moon outside creeping through the curtains. He knew the layout of the room anyway, they were all the same. But he waited until he could see the outlines of the walls and furniture so that he wouldn't bump into anything. More importantly, he listened hard. As he hoped, he heard the sound of someone breathing in and out from a deep sleep under the covers on the bed. He stepped once towards the corner of the bed and waited again. The sleeper didn't move or change breathing pattern so he hadn't been heard.

Shuffling two steps sideways along the side of the bed towards the headboard, the man noticed the person in the bed was the woman he was expecting to be there, lying on her left side under a duvet and facing away from him with her legs tucked up towards her waist. Good. Less chance of a struggle. He pulled a small bottle from his left trouser pocket and unscrewed the lid. From his right pocket he took out a handkerchief and poured the contents of the bottle onto it, putting the bottle back into his left pocket. He turned to his left and bent forwards so he was in line with the sleeping woman's body. He leaned over her and hovered his right hand, carrying the soaked hanky, over her head. Then in one movement he lifted his right leg and straddled her hips with all his weight while at the same time pushing her head into the pillow with his left hand and clamping the hanky over her mouth and nose with his right.

In the space of four or five seconds, Lucy woke with a start from a deep sleep, felt a heavy weight pressing her down into the mattress, tried to wriggle free, gasped for air and then succumbed to the chemical vapour on whatever was covering her face.

The man in the white uniform was half as heavy again as

Lucy, and despite her efforts, had no problem keeping her held down for a few seconds until she fell unconscious. Now he just had to get her out of the room without anyone noticing.

Chapter 68

On Deck Nine a wheelchair sat outside the door of room number 9148. When the door opened, a man in an engineer's uniform slipped out quietly and ran around the back of the chair, pulling it back slightly, so the man that followed him, carrying a small middle-aged woman who appeared to be asleep, could deposit her into the chair. The woman's head lolled to one side as she was propped up. The first man took a blanket out of a pocket on the back of the chair and wedged it around the woman. The second man stood back in the doorway and let the first man push the wheelchair away down the corridor, then he closed the door silently, turned and walked the opposite way.

In the room across the corridor Barker turned over in his sleep.

Chapter 69

Lucy's head was pounding and she could hardly move. She managed to open her eyes a little, but in the darkness she was disorientated and didn't understand what was going on. She could see a figure opening her wardrobe and rifling through her clothes on the rails, but who could that be? What time was it? Nothing made any sense, but she knew something was wrong and tried to work out what she could do. She couldn't attack him. She felt so heavy. Then she saw a small handbag on the bedside table and began to drag herself across the bed. The man in the wardrobe had his back to her and was making enough noise not to notice as she edged further across. Lucy got to the far edge of the bed nearest the window and made a desperate lunge with her right arm to grab the handbag, falling out of the bed and onto the floor, scattering the contents.

The man turned around when he heard the bang and threw the dress he was holding onto the bed and ran round to the other side, where he saw Lucy instinctively trying to get up. He stood astride her, sat down across her waist, pinning her down on her back, and took out the handkerchief he used before and pressed it across her nose and mouth. Unable to resist, Lucy fell into unconsciousness again.

Chapter 70

Barker wasn't a heavy sleeper, especially since he'd been living alone. Laura had imposed a rule that cell phones weren't allowed in their bedroom because of all the notifications he would get at all hours, disturbing their sleep. On the ship he had no choice but to have it in the room, but in the middle of the Atlantic it was unlikely to receive anything so he'd reluctantly left it on his bedside table. So when it pinged in the middle of the night and woke him from a light doze, he wondered if it was just telling him it was low on charge. He rolled over intending to turn it off so he could attempt to get some sleep and glanced at a notification on the screen.

Margaret Gibson – Atrium, Deck Five

"What? Why is that there?" He sat up in the dark with the screen lighting his face and swiped to unlock the phone. The ship's Sea Star app opened up and told him the latest location of Margaret Gibson, apparently travelling through the Atrium.

"At four-fifteen in the morning?" said Barker to himself. "Who is Margaret Gibson anyway, and why do I need to know?"

The fog in his half-asleep mind cleared slowly and locked onto the fact that he and Lucy had been in a stateroom in the name of 'Gibson' the previous night, and he couldn't help feeling a little flutter of panic. He sat up straighter and stared at the screen again when it clicked up another notification.

Margaret Gibson – Emporium, Deck Five

"So now she's going shopping."

Barker twisted out from under his covers and sat on the edge of the bed and switched on the lamp on the table next to him, bathing the room in a soft warm white glow, and tried to work out what this meant and whether he should be worried. It could be a coincidence couldn't it? There could be more than one Gibson on the ship, surely? But why would it be alerting him? How had Margaret Gibson's Sea Star been registered to his phone?

"Lucy!" Barker's mind cleared in an instant and he remembered Lucy going through a handbag in the Gibson stateroom. She'd picked out the competition ticket and given it to him, then gone through some of the other bits and pieces. Like a typical man he had shut his mind to what else was in the handbag, but she could easily have picked up Margaret's Sea Star and kept it. When they'd got back to her room afterwards, she'd asked Barker for his cell phone and he'd thought nothing of it. She must've registered it then.

Barker took a swig of water out of the glass on the table next to the bed, stood up and grabbed some spare clothes from a pile on the sofa and put them on.

Chapter 71

Lucy's head throbbed as she slowly drifted into consciousness from a deep sleep. As thoughts began to form in her mind she wondered why she was so tired. Had she been drinking the night before? What else would explain the banging headache? If it hadn't been for that, she thought, she could just drift off back to sleep and wait until she was feeling fresher. Obviously, waking now wasn't a good idea. Her body wasn't ready. Then she wondered if she'd overslept and that possibility shot enough adrenaline through her veins to make it impossible to drift off again until she could wake and check the time.

She could hear noises nearby. Not outside in the corridors, but inside the room. They were unfamiliar, muffled, occasional noises that didn't make any sense. She tried to open her eyes but didn't succeed. Everything was dark. She felt cold, not like she was in her warm bed under the duvet. Her shoulders were bare, and her feet felt wrong, like she was wearing shoes. In bed? Her mind was clearing slowly and a chink of light crept in at the bottom of her vision, but she still couldn't open her eyes properly. It felt like her eyelids were moving but nothing was happening.

Lucy suddenly realised that the noise was voices, and the memory of the man in her room shocked her awake with a jolt.

She seemed to be sat down with her back against something, a wall maybe, or the bed where she'd fallen? What was she wearing? Where was this? She was slumped, but as she woke, she wriggled and tried to sit up. Then she realised her hands were tied together behind her back and she couldn't support herself, so slid sideways to her left onto the floor.

One of the voices got closer and the words began to clear. She felt a presence in front of her and a pair of hands on her shoulders lifted her back upright and then moved to her feet and stretched them straight out in front of her. More comfortable but no less confused.

"Where...what going?" Lucy managed, still coming round.

"Ah, there you are," said another voice coming from a different direction than the owner of the hands that had helped her. "I thought I'd overdone it and finished you off. That wasn't in the plan. I hope you're OK. You'll feel better soon."

The voice was close to her, somewhere on her left side, and down at her level now, as if someone – a man - was crouching next to her.

"After all, we need you. You're the key to the next phase."

The voice was familiar but her head wasn't straight yet and she couldn't place him.

"I'm sorry it worked out this way Lucy. You got mixed up in something that's not your fault."

Then it clicked in Lucy's brain. "Michael?"

"Ah, there she is.' The voice replied, "Back in the land of the living."

"What the hell Michael? Where am I? What are you doing to me?"

"You, my friend, are chief liaison officer. All part of the plan."

"Chief what? What plan? Was it you in my room last night?"

"Yes, it was me. It was a bit trickier than I thought, but I got you here in the end. Nobody saw us, but I had my cover story ready just in case. A woman who'd had a few too many being carried to safety by an officer. Nobody would have thought anything of it. I even got you dressed for the occasion."

Lucy could tell she was wearing some sort of dress that felt familiar and must've stuck a pair of heels on her feet as he'd carried her from her room to wherever they were now.

"Could've put a bra on me!" she shouted indignantly, but shuddered, "On second thoughts, maybe not."

"Nothing I haven't seen before Lucy," Michael replied.

"Piss off!" Lucy shouted but flinched as a hard slap hit her left cheek and she gasped for air.

"You're not in a position to be abusive here Lucy. I don't want to hurt anyone, but you're going to have to do what you're told. I'll have someone fetch you a coffee to help you come round and then maybe you'll feel a bit more helpful."

Chapter 72

Barker walked down the corridor from his room wearing a mixed collection of clothes he'd dumped on his sofa the day before. Trousers and shoes, no socks. No time. He did grab a thin jumper, in case he had to walk outside at some point. They might be on their way to the Caribbean, he thought, but it's still cold at night in the middle of the Atlantic.

He came to the midships staircase and headed up to Deck Five where the last notification had told him Margaret Gibson had been. As he did so, another one pinged on his phone:

Margaret Gibson – Explorers Lounge, Deck Five

The Explorers Lounge was a little further on than the Emporium, the designer shops onboard where the cruise company helped passengers part with more of their money. The Atrium was well lit and Barker noted how different it was in the middle of the night without all the people and the hubbub. He would have stopped for a look around if he hadn't had more on his mind. As he walked down the corridor past the Emporium he noticed a maintenance man on a stepladder changing lightbulbs in the ceiling.

"Good morning sir," said the man politely.

"Morning," replied Barker with a polite smile as he slipped past.

Barker walked quickly but with his eyes scanning as far ahead as he could in case he saw anything untoward, but he didn't know what to expect. It could be a wild goose chase, but he was worried enough to have got up in the middle of the night to go looking for Lucy.

Margaret Gibson – Adriatic Suite, Deck Five

Barker's pulse quickened at the new notification, as he realised it was the location of their meeting the previous morning, and where they had arranged to meet the others again later today. In his mind this made it more likely that it wasn't just an innocent coincidence, and that he could be being led into a trap. He stopped for a second. Maybe it wasn't Lucy he was following at all. Maybe it was the killer. Had he killed Margaret as well, and stolen her Sea Star, to fool Barker into following him? He decided to carry on carefully and look for escape routes as he went.

Chapter 73

Lucy twitched as she felt a pair of hands around the back of her head undoing the blindfold that had kept her in the dark until now. They weren't Michael's hands. They belonged to the person who had helped her sit up and straightened her legs before, a Hispanic man in an engineer's overalls, with the Galaxy logo – a crew member, but not one she recognised.

The light in the room seemed blinding at first, but she blinked and adjusted quickly and looked uncertainly around the room. There were other people sat on the floor around the perimeter, with blindfolds and hands tied behind their backs. It took her a few seconds to recognise some of them from the meeting the previous morning: Janet, Jordan and Sam were there, plus a couple of faces she didn't know.

A young Asian woman walked over to her carrying a cup of coffee and squatted down in front of her, offering the cup up to her mouth to take a sip.

"Jas…Jasmine?" whispered Lucy, recognising the girl from the meeting, "What are you…? What's going on?"

"Drink up. I will help." Jasmine replied.

"Why am I here Jasmine? What have I done?"

Jasmine just looked blankly into Lucy's eyes and offered the cup again. Lucy accepted that she wasn't going to answer and took a sip of the lukewarm coffee, hoping it would clear her head.

"More," Jasmine said, tipping the cup again. Lucy took a couple more mouthfuls and said, "Thank you." Jasmine pulled away, stood up and walked across the room without looking back. She put the cup down on a table by the entrance to the room which Lucy recognised now as the one they'd held the meeting in the day before. Michael was stood talking to another man who seemed to be guarding the door. The man nodded as Michael gave him instructions, and then Michael turned to face the room.

"Now that we have Lucy we can move on. Miss Jones is going to help us achieve our goal," Michael said, looking around the room at each of the captive passengers.

Lucy stared at the man she'd once admired and now hated, trying to fight the impulse to shout obscenities at him, and instead asked the question on everyone's lips, "Did you kill all those people?"

Michael turned his gaze to Lucy, fixing his eyes on hers and said, "No."

"So who did?"

"Somebody desperate to spoil my plan."

"So what do you want us for?" a voice interrupted. It was Janet, mild-mannered Janet. "Why are we here if she's the one you need?" said Janet avoiding eye contact with Lucy.

"I brought you all here to keep you safe," said Michael.

"Ha!" shouted one of the hostages from under his gag. Michael ignored him.

"Laugh if you want but somebody is killing your friends, and you would likely be next if I hadn't brought you here. All that matters is that Lucy can help us end this peacefully."

"I have no idea what you're talking about," said Lucy, "What's it got to do with me?"

"It's not you. It's your father I need. But you're going to speak to him for me."

Shaken at the mention of her father, Lucy gulped and said, "I haven't spoken to my father in four years."

"Well you're about to have a reconciliation."

Chapter 74

"What's my father got to do with anything?" Lucy questioned her captor.

Michael slowly walked towards Lucy, "Your father is the reason I went to jail. Your father isn't the angel you think he is."

"I don't think he's an angel. He kicked me out at sixteen."

"Well, that's what he does. He gets rid of things he doesn't need or want. But I'm hoping he has enough affection left for you that he'll do what I need him to."

"And what's that?"

"Pay me twenty million dollars."

Lucy's mouth dropped open. "Why would he do that?"

"Because that's what he stole from me."

"Stole?"

"Yes, stole. That money was mine until he took it and left me to rot. He could have helped. He could have walked away, but he took it like it belonged to him. Now I want it back, and he's in a position to pay."

"And you think he'll give you twenty million for me? I doubt it."

"Probably not, but I have his ship. He's a majority shareholder in the company that owns Starlight."

Lucy was stunned, she had no idea. She knew her father owned a cargo shipping company, but not that he'd branched out into cruise ships. She couldn't find a reply.

Michael continued, "So I have his ship, his daughter, and these good people here who are all related in some way to members of the board of ABJ Transatlantic. I invited them all here so I could use them to get my money back. But then somebody started killing them, which is no good to me is it? A ransom demand without hostages doesn't work."

Lucy managed just one word, "Who...?"

"I don't know," said Michael.

"I'm sure you've made enemies."

"Probably. But it's not important. What's important is getting my money back."

Chapter 75

Barker walked down the last small corridor of staterooms before it came to an end at the ship's spa and treatment rooms, which were next to the Adriatic Suite conference room. He'd got used to the constant buzz of a cruise ship, never quiet, always people around, but now, here, it was silent, apart from the occasional buzz of an electric light or air conditioning unit. He could feel the ship gently rolling from side to side as it ploughed on through the dark ocean. As he walked he strained his hearing to search for any sounds in front or behind him but heard nothing apart from the occasional snoring passenger in their stateroom.

The corridor ahead of him soon became the spa reception area, but opened up on the left into the familiar lobby outside the Adriatic suite. Barker stood for a second and looked around before quickly and quietly sprinting across the ship to the opposite corridor to check if there was anyone there. Satisfied he was alone he walked back over to the Adriatic Suite door, trying to remember which way it would open if someone suddenly left the room, giving him a couple of seconds cover to run or hide. He put his right ear up against the door, feeling a little bit ridiculous. All those years of police training and experience and it boiled down to listening through a wall.

There were voices, muffled and unintelligible, but definitely people talking in the room. But how many and was one of them Lucy? Was she even there? Suddenly, he heard a voice much clearer and louder, obviously close to the door. Barker jumped back and swung around towards the spa reception just as the handle of the Adriatic Suite door moved downwards and the door swung slowly open. He managed to run into the reception area and hide behind a pillar just inside. He was convinced they must have heard him, but quiet footsteps came towards him and swung to his left into the corridor that he'd just come down. Just as he let out his breath as the footsteps faded, his body was slammed up against the pillar and a hand came round the right side of his face and clamped across his mouth. Another hand came around his left side and across his stomach and began shuffling him backwards deeper into the spa, through a door and into one of the treatment rooms.

Barker was spun around and released into the corner of the room. Heart racing, he looked up to face his attacker and prepared himself for what might come next. With a mixture of relief and exasperation, he found himself staring again at Maria Cortez.

"What the fuck are you doing? I thought I told you to keep out of it!" whispered Maria forcefully.

Barker just shook his head and looked at the floor as he took a few deep breaths and let his heart start to slow down.

"Are you determined to get yourself killed?"

"Why would I get killed? I thought you said you didn't know what was going on? I'm trying to help Lucy. She's in there."

"Do you know that for sure? Do you know she's in there? It doesn't matter anyway. If you step through those doors you're involved and you're dead."

"And what about you? Why are you here? Couldn't you be in trouble too? You're sneaking around the place just like me."

"I'm *bringing* trouble John. He doesn't know it yet. But he will."

"You owe me an explanation Maria. You need to tell me what you know."

"I don't owe you anything John, but...sit down," said Maria, gesturing at the padded treatment table in the middle of the room. She moved across to the solitary chair in the room and sat down herself, sighing a little as she did so.

"My friend is in there. He's taken her, I'm sure of it." Barker continued.

"Your girlfriend?"

"My...does it matter? She's in danger."

"Ok John, I'll tell you. At least what I know." Maria took a deep breath, looked up at John, and continued. "Michael Brennan is my ex-husband. That's not his real name...at least it wasn't when I was married to him. Actually, I think I still am married to him, but anyway...he's a drug runner, has been for fifteen years. He was in the navy before, so he knew his way around ships and started shipping cocaine out of Colombia using vessels belonging to a cargo company he had gone to work for as cover. It went wrong, he got caught and went to jail."

Barker took this in before asking, "So what's that got to do with you? Why are you here?"

"I'm here for revenge John," Maria said matter-of-factly.

Barker looked at her, puzzled. Maria continued, "I know what you're going to say John. Did I know about it? Yes, I did. So sue me. I had a tough upbringing John, we had nothing. I met a man who took me out of that world and helped my family. I didn't know where his money came from at first but I knew it was business dealings, probably not legal. So I went along with it for a while. He gave me two beautiful children. He got a trophy wife. I'm not proud of him, but I did what I had to do."

"And...?" said Barker, taking it all in.

"And it all went to shit, as it always does in that world. Violence never goes away. It just spreads. I was naïve. I thought I could live on the sidelines and it wouldn't affect me but it did. My family got involved. My brother...my stupid brother got himself into it and got killed. Michael could have stopped him, but didn't."

"So that's why you've come for Michael?"

"Yes and no. My brother knew what he was getting into and I should have done too. Just before he got caught I told Michael I wanted out...out of that lifestyle. If that meant leaving him I was prepared to do that but I asked him to come with me and give it all up. We had a comfortable life, we could be happy for a long time. But no, he couldn't do that. Money is addictive and the numbers kept getting bigger. So he had me killed."

"What?" said Barker, confused.

"From his prison cell, before his trial, he arranged for someone to track me down and kill me, so I wouldn't be able to say anything."

"I'm not following."

"Most of his heavies are just thugs, idiots who are just as greedy as the rest. The man he sent was...distracted... by me and my money. He came at dawn and broke into our house. Michael had told him how to bypass our security. He got into my room while I was asleep and attacked me. He climbed on top of me and tied me up. I'm sure he would've raped me if my son hadn't heard him and walked into the room. Instead he grabbed Julio and stopped him from screaming, then helped himself to my jewellery and cash. I told him to just take it and leave my children alone. But he took..."

Maria's eyes began to glisten and her hard edge began to crack.

"He took Julio. He said 'He's tough, He will make a good fighter. He's one of us now.'"

"I'm sorry," said Barker

Maria took a deep breath, straightened up a little and continued. "He told me what Michael had asked him to do, but that he didn't want to kill anyone. So I should disappear, and that if I didn't, he would kill Julio."

"And your other child?" Barker asked.

"Emily? She is safe. I made her disappear with me."

"So why are you here now? Isn't that putting yourself and Julio in danger? And why have you been out in public on the ship? I mean you're an attractive woman...you..." Barker stopped himself briefly, blushing as he caught Maria's eye, "... you don't... blend into the background."

"Julio was eight when they took him," Maria continued, "Michael's trial took a year, and he was inside for three and has been out for two more. So he would be fourteen now."

"Would be," she'd said. Barker sensed what was coming next.

"His body was found a year ago. At first I didn't understand. I had kept quiet, started a new life, as painful as it was without my son. But I did it for Emily, to keep her safe. Julio got into a gang. He was shot in a gunfight, crossfire. He wasn't even carrying a weapon."

Barker couldn't think of anything to say. 'Sorry' didn't

seem enough. He just looked at Maria, whose hard edge had returned, and sighed. They looked at each other for a few seconds, absorbing this story.

"So now you know why I'm here. That bastard is why my son is dead. It's taken me this long to track them down."

"Them?" asked Barker.

"Yes, 'them'. Two for the price of one. I came looking for Michael and found the man who took Julio. Working in the fucking kitchens would you believe? He took hundreds of thousands of dollars from my home and he's working in a cruise ship kitchen. That's when I knew that something must be happening on this ship. At first, I didn't want to 'blend into the background', I wanted Michael to see me, to get that shock. But when I saw Jaime Vega I knew I had to step back and deal with it differently. So I dealt with him first."

Chapter 76

Lucy sat on a padded metal chair at a table near the door of the Adriatic Suite and watched Jasmine tie her ankles to the legs of the chair so she couldn't make a run for it. Jasmine then went behind her and cut the ties on her wrists so they were free. Michael handed her the cup of coffee she'd sipped from earlier and told her to drink it. Reluctantly she did. Her mouth was dry and she was still waking up so the coffee at least was welcome, even if the situation wasn't.

"Now take this and ring this number," Michael instructed her, handing Lucy a satellite phone and a piece of paper.

"And what if he puts the phone down when he hears it's me?" said Lucy.

"We'll ring him again," replied Michael, "And explain the predicament you're in."

Lucy dialled the number and listened to the faint dial tone, hoping no one would answer. She knew her father was based in London, so although it was the middle of the night on the ship, it was early morning in England. He was an early riser and early to work, and always had a phone in his pocket. She'd no idea if this was his number, as she'd long since stopped trying to contact him but...

"Hello? Who is this?" a voice said suspiciously. Lucy

shivered. She'd resigned herself to never speaking to him again so had never prepared for this moment. She decided to stick to the facts.

"It's me Dad. It's Lucy." She braced herself for a reply. "Dad?" she said, after a long silence."

"I heard you. What do you want?" said Aidan Jones...on loudspeaker.

"I'm in trouble Dad."

"You're always in trouble."

"Yes but..."

"But this time it's real trouble Aidan. Are you well?" Michael interrupted.

Another long pause. "Who is this?"

"You know who it is Aidan. We're old friends."

"But you're in..."

"In prison, yes, I was. But I got out. Easy when you know how. Or who. Anyway I'm sat here with Lucy on a ship in the middle of the Atlantic ocean, in the middle of the night. She's tied to her chair..."

"I don't give a damn about Lucy. She knows that. The feeling's mutual. She..."

"I want my money Aidan. You know how much and you know why. I have your daughter, and if you don't care about that I have the relatives of your board members here too. I've sent you an email with a nice group photo for proof and I've copied everyone in. You probably won't recognise them because you won't know them personally, but you should be getting phone calls to confirm that very soon. All you have to do is transfer twenty million to my account and they'll all get home safely. Otherwise...they won't. And neither will this ship. I know you sunk a lot of cash into the launch of this cruise line Aidan, so if

I get my money I'll let you keep your ship and your company's reputation. If not, you'll lose it all. You've got one hour."

"Don't you try to..." Click. Michael ended the call.

Chapter 77

"We need to get out of here," said Barker, looking at his watch, "It's five O'clock and the staff will be coming in soon."

"We can't go together in case we're spotted," replied Maria. "I'll go first, back to my room. You follow in five minutes. Room number 5237. Don't get caught."

"What about Lucy?"

"He needs her. She's safe. For now."

Maria opened the door of the treatment room and, after a pause to look around, slipped out of sight leaving the door slightly ajar. Barker stood up and closed the door behind her and waited. He did like Lucy. And the thought of her life being in danger took his thoughts back to Laura. He'd managed to shake off the depression in the last few days with so much going on and Lucy to distract him. But now the hurt was back, along with fear. Fear that he might lose her as well.

Ten minutes later, Barker tapped quietly on the door of 5237. Maria opened it instantly, as if she'd been stood right by it waiting for him.

"Come in," she said, ushering him into the large, warm suite, four or five times the size of his own pokey little stateroom. "I've ordered breakfast. It'll be here soon. Take a seat."

Barker wasn't sure where to sit. Normally there isn't much choice in a stateroom: the bed or the chair. But in this huge suite there were separate lounge and dining rooms. He walked across to a sofa and sat down. Maria followed with two cups of coffee and sat next to him. Despite her hard exterior, Barker could see that she was looking tired, or just upset that she'd had to re-live everything in order to bring him up to speed. It was good to finally get behind the mask and get to know the real Maria Cortez, and that they were both on the same side.

"You...er...you killed him?" Barker ventured, "The man that took your son?" turning to his right and looking at Maria.

Maria sat back on the sofa, kicked off her shoes, and put her feet up on the coffee table in front of them, visibly relaxing with every sip of coffee, now that they were safe.

"Yes." Maria turned and looked Barker in the eye as if to plead with him to believe her. "He took my son."

"I'm sure I would've done the same."

"You have children?"

"No. No, but I can imagine...my wife didn't want..."

"I'm sorry..."

There was a knock at the door. Maria got up and looked through the spyglass: breakfast.

A well-dressed waiter wearing white gloves pushed in a trolley piled high with every breakfast item Barker could imagine, then transferred everything to the dining table and left them alone.

"Help yourself." Maria gestured with a smile.

Taking a few plates over to the coffee table, they sat back down again and began to eat.

"You say Michael 'got caught'? Doing what?"

"Shipping cocaine. He'd done it dozens of times before. I don't know how, or who, but somebody tipped off the coastguard and they came looking. Michael had a backup plan to transfer it all to another boat, a fast one. They'd transferred most of the cargo when the captain of the smaller boat got spooked and left or, as Michael believes, was told to leave without him, making sure he took the rap. The coastguard picked him up with what was left of the consignment. It was enough to have him put away. The first I knew about it was a call from his lawyer."

"So you went into hiding?"

"Not immediately no. I had no reason to believe we were in danger until the lawyer told me Michael didn't want to speak to me. That worried me. A week or so later Vega broke into our house."

After a pause and a deep sigh, Barker said, "So what do you know about what happened to my wife?"

Maria looked away from him and down at her food. "John, I shouldn't..."

"You said they'd already hurt someone close to me."

"That's not what I said."

"It's what you meant. You also said 'He shouldn't have sent you' What did you mean? Do you mean Rob?"

Maria paused, "Not everyone is what you think they are John. Some people work for both sides. Or just for themselves."

Barker closed his eyes and sighed. "If he hurt my wife I'll kill him."

"No John. I don't think so. I can't be sure but he was just for information. Not for that. Someone else..."

"Your husband?"

"Maybe. Not personally, but..."

Barker stared at Maria. "Why?"

"I don't know details. A shipment was seized on the Thames. Michael said forensics would be brought in and panicked. He must have got details of the lab from Rob and..."

"OK, I get it."

Now it was Barker's turn to look away and stare into space, breathing deeply. "So we have to deal with him. With *them*."

Chapter 78

Aidan Jones' cell phone rang again, about two minutes after Michael had cut their conversation short.

Diane Collins

"Diane. Good morning. How are..." began Aidan, just in case the call was a coincidence.

"What have you done Aidan?! What the hell..!" Diane shouted.

"Calm down Diane, I can..."

"Calm fucking down?! I've just brought my son home in a box and you tell me to calm down now that someone tells me it's your fault?!"

"It's blackmail Diane, I'm being blackmailed."

Aidan's landline started to ring and there was a knock at his office door.

"Don't talk shit Aidan, I've known you too long. This has got your name all over it."

"What has? Diane, I don't know what you're..."

"Drugs, Aidan. Drugs. I can't believe you'd stoop so low, and yet I know it's true. You've always had it in you to do something like this."

"Diane, I didn't..." Click. Diane hung up. The landline was still ringing and Jones' PA opened the door and said, "Aidan

I've got Stephen Mitchell on the line for you. I think you'd better answer. He's very upset."

Just as he was about to pick up, Jones' personal cell phone rang. He fished it out of his jacket pocket.

Helen Gibson

"Helen. I..." Jones began.

Helen said, "Don't speak Aidan. Just listen. We're on our way. And you'd better be there when we get there," and ended the call.

Jones' head was starting to spin, but he picked up the ringing landline. "Stephen, hello. It's..."

"I'm shaking Aidan. I've just had a call from David Howarth, Samantha's son. Apparently, he's just received an email with a photo attached showing eight people tied up and terrified. Two days Aidan and we didn't even know about it. What the hell is going on? And what have you done? And what about Jack? If that's got something to do with you Aidan I swear to God I'll..."

"Stephen, don't..."

"I'm coming over now Aidan. Don't you dare leave."

Chapter 79

Outside, the morning was sunny and clear and Starlight was within twenty-five miles of her last port of call at Nassau in the Bahamas before her final destination of Fort Lauderdale in Florida. The sea was fairly calm and other than a light breeze the weather was idyllic. Consequently, the early risers were starting to appear on deck. The crew had long been up and about cleaning and preparing the Skyscape restaurant and cafes dotted about the place. And now their customers were beginning to appear.

Elderly people and families with young children were usually the first to go for breakfast, as well as those staying in Starlight's few inside staterooms where there was no natural light, making them want to get up and out as soon as possible. In many ways this was the best time to eat because the displays were full of freshly-prepared food and there weren't yet any crowds. Empty tables were plentiful so no one had to struggle to find one for long, and the queues at the counters were short.

Meanwhile, most of those of working age that were travelling without kids were probably still in bed, making the most of the luxury of no alarm clock and enjoying their brief respite from the daily grind. They would come for breakfast later, boosting the queues and searching for places to sit. Some of them would skip breakfast altogether and instead go for an early lunch.

Out by the pool, the first wave of dedicated sun worshippers were reserving loungers with towels and paperbacks and sometimes a trustingly-left bag of paraphernalia such as hats, sunglasses and cream to block the worst of the sun's rays. Some of them would then join the others in the restaurant for breakfast while a few would start their sunbathing early and open their paperback or Kindle and lay back on their loungers and enjoy the relative peace. In an hour or two there would be few loungers left. The couples and families and children would fill the pool and the teenagers would all meet in the hot tubs at either side.

Inside the ship a steady flow of people were waking up and wandering out of their rooms via lifts and staircases into the public spaces, sometimes with no other purpose than to see what everyone else was doing and enjoy the relaxed atmosphere. The theatre was closed for cleaning and rehearsals, and the bars were deserted except for a few die-hard early-starters.

Chapter 80

In the Adriatic Suite, Michael picked his cell phone off the table and dialled Aidan Jones' number, barely an hour after cutting his last call off. It rang and rang with no answer, so he ended the call. Michael paced up and down impatiently for a few seconds, staring at Lucy, who stared back.

"You'd better hope he comes good Lucy, for all our sakes," said Michael, turning and looking at the other hostages.

"Not a lot I can do about it if he doesn't," Lucy replied, "He loves money more than he loves me. You obviously didn't do your homework."

Michael started to walk towards Lucy but his cell phone rang before he got close.

"Aidan. I thought you were avoiding me," Michael said.

"I'm not paying Michael." Aidan replied, "You're not getting anything."

Michael paused and breathed in and out, deeply. And angrily. "Not even to save your little girl Aidan?"

Lucy's ears pricked at the mention of her and the implications of what she'd heard.

"That's very foolish of you Aidan. Don't you believe I'm capable of it? After all we went through setting this operation up? After I've spent three years in a Colombian jail? Do you think I'm too weak? Or are you trying to call my bluff? Do I need to make my point?"

"I can't give in to terrorism Michael. You're just an angry man who made the wrong choices and now wants to blame everybody else. The world can't give in to that every time someone like you demands it. My daughter will have told you by now that her being there won't make a difference to..." Click. Michael cut Jones off and threw his phone across the room, smashing off the wall above the head of one of the terrified hostages, his face twisted with frustration.

"The board can't have got to him yet. I should have given them more time. They'll change his mind. Meanwhile, I'll give them something else to think about."

Chapter 81

Daryl and Rose Jackson from Ohio were lucky. They'd always felt they were blessed with good luck. They had a happy, healthy family, loving children and a couple of grandchildren all doing well and in good health. They didn't ask for much out of life: just a comfortable home, enough money to live on and a couple of holidays a year, maybe more when Daryl retires next year. Their kids had done well at school, got good jobs, and were in a position to look after their parents if ever that was required.

Last night Rose's numbers came up on the bingo competition and Daryl won at the tables in the casino. They never spent big and stuck to their budget – sometimes they won, sometimes they lost, but they budgeted for it as part of their holiday. This time though, they could pay for next year's holidays. Eighteen thousand dollars all told. Now that's lucky.

Luckier still was the fact that they'd forgotten Rose's camera when they left their room to go for breakfast. She liked to take it with her wherever they went so she could record her day on video. So they turned around and went back down two levels to their room. Lucky because just as they closed their door behind them they heard a piercing whistle from their in-room speaker lasting a couple of seconds, followed by another, then five more. A final, longer blast meant this was the ship's general emergency signal and as there hadn't been an announcement before, it was not an exercise.

Daryl and Rose were rooted to the spot, bracing themselves against the noise. They were lucky because the first thing they were expected to do in the event of an emergency was to go to their stateroom and collect their life jackets, before going to their allocated Muster Station for further instructions. They had always been told this alarm didn't necessarily mean they would have to abandon ship, but they'd never believed that. They'd always worried if this ever happened whether they'd get back to their stateroom fast enough to get their life jackets before panic set in and the corridors got crowded with frantic passengers.

"That's was lucky," said Daryl.

Chapter 82

On the Lido Deck the early birds who had claimed their sun loungers before most of the rest of the passengers had finished breakfast were looking at each other in confusion as the general alarm signal finished its seven short blasts and one longer one.

"Was that an exercise?" Could be heard around the deck as people absorbed what they'd heard. "What's the problem?" someone muttered.

The sky was clear and blue, the sea was calm, there were no other ships visible. Nobody could fathom what was going on. On the horizon, you could just make out a faintly craggy line indicating land after days of endless sea. They were due to dock in Nassau later that morning but nobody had thought to look for land just yet. What they were just beginning to notice as they got up and looked around the ship's sides was that they were travelling extremely slowly. Someone said, "I think we're slowing down."

Quite often in a morning, if there was time in the schedule, the ship would slow down while the majority of people had their first meal of the day. If time needed making up then the captain could always do that once it went dark, during dinner in the evening or overnight. But the ship was indeed slowing down. In fact, the engines had been shut down. The wake at the back of the ship, carefully engineered to minimise vibration under normal circumstances, was disappearing altogether as the ship coasted without power. It would be a good few minutes yet before it stopped altogether. But that was the plan.

Passengers began streaming out of the Skyscape restaurant through the Lido Deck, to get to their staterooms as quickly as they could. Most of the people around the pool had stood up and begun to gather their belongings so they could head back too, and pick up their life jackets on the way to their muster stations. A few diehards had decided it must be an exercise and they simply must have misheard it, and chose to stay right where they were and make the most of the sun.

The corridors inside the ship were gradually filling up. Like commuters getting off a train in rush hour and walking along the platform, people appeared from doorways and strode purposefully down their corridor towards their rooms. The noise level was rising and people chatted with their partners, families and complete strangers to reassure or compare theories as to what it might all be about. Nobody had seen or heard a collision, the weather was good, so spirits were still high as nobody felt in real danger.

In the theatre at the front of the ship the seats were beginning to fill as the crew directed passengers and gave polite but vague answers to the question, 'What's happening?' The truth was they didn't know. They were in the dark like everyone else but had noticed the engines had stopped. They would do their jobs as they'd been trained and wait for further instructions.

At their muster station in the main dining room at the aft end of the ship, Daryl and Rose walked in and found a seat and began to put on their life jackets. Rose had grabbed her camera even though it was beginning to look like she wasn't going to be using it any time soon. Through the windows at the side of the ship, Daryl could see some crew members marching along the promenade deck and climbing up onto a lifeboat and opening the door. He wasn't the only one that noticed. His heart began to beat a little faster as he realised for the first time this might be for real.

Chapter 83

Barker and Maria were thinking about going back out when they heard the alarm whistle.

"What now?" said Barker.

"No idea, but I don't like it," replied Maria.

"We have to go back and see what's going on in that room. Why would they..."

"Calm down John. It's probably a diversion. They might want to move those people and take advantage of the confusion."

"How long will it take to get everyone to their muster stations?"

"Less than you might think. You missed the full drill at the beginning of the cruise – it's very well organised. Half an hour maximum."

"That's when they'll move them. Everyone will be out of their way."

"Or it might be a genuine emergency."

"Too much of a coincidence. We need to find out what's going on in that room. What's on the other side of it?"

"Other side of what?"

"The conference room. Can we get close to it any other way?"

"There's the sanctuary at that end, next to the spa. It's a quiet, adults-only area. We could take a look."

The corridor outside was beginning to fill with people returning to their staterooms to retrieve their life jackets and go to their Muster stations.

"We need to go now," said Maria. "Once they start counting heads and realise we're not at our muster station they'll come looking for us."

Barker was halfway out of the door before she'd finished her sentence.

Chapter 84

In the Atrium, all four decks were filling with passengers carrying life-jackets and looking for somewhere to sit. Each of the floors was a designated Muster Station for a certain group of passengers, usually from the staterooms on that same level. In normal everyday use these spaces would never cater for this many people, so every available chair was taken and people were standing in every gap in between. Each person had their Sea Star scanned in through each doorway to be sure everyone was present, and the crew members were directing people away from the lifts and into the staircases.

The mood was one of nervous excitement. Some passengers had spied the land on the horizon so were confident of being rescued quickly if it came to it, but many were quite worried. The elderly and infirm sat in their chairs or wheelchairs looking around them hoping the evacuation would go smoothly and not put them at too much risk. The majority of passengers would have been on board the lifeboats when they were used as tenders to reach some of the ports where a cruise ship jetty wasn't available. This could be because of a lack of a developed jetty in a poorer destination, or simply too many ships arriving on the same day. But the tenders required a degree of mobility to step onto from the door in Starlight's side at sea level. A degree of mobility that roughly ten percent of the guests didn't have. They would have to rely on the crew being well trained to get them safely into a lifeboat, before they could begin to relax.

Through the windows at the sides of the ship, the passengers could see that Starlight had virtually stopped moving. The sea was a little choppy from the breeze but nothing that moved the 115,000-tonne cruise ship. Conditions couldn't really have been much better.

"Ladies and gentlemen, could I please have your attention?" came a voice over a loudspeaker. The voice belonged to Kirsty, a member of the entertainment team – a familiar face to reassure people. "Thank you for your cooperation so far, we're all accounted for in the Atrium Muster Stations now. As you are all aware there has been a general alarm signal sent by the captain. First thing to say is that there is no damage to the ship so we are not going to sink." Kirsty smiled and paused for almost a thousand people to breathe a collective sigh of relief.

"However, we are told that the ship has no power and is coming to a stop which, as you've probably noticed will not be long now. It's too deep to anchor here so the ship will be drifting. So for safety, as were are just eighteen miles from Nassau we will evacuate passengers and non-essential crew from the ship and head to the port." Kirsty paused again for the inevitable chatter. "This is a big operation and will take time, but with your help and patience it will go very smoothly and everyone will be taken to their lifeboat safely. Pay attention to the crew members nearest to you and follow their instructions. Thanks for your help and we'll see you in port very soon."

Chapter 85

Barker was ten yards ahead of Maria by the time she grabbed her shoes and got out of the door and followed. The corridor was filling up with people going in both directions, some carrying life jackets, others looking for their rooms. She could see Barker ahead and was surprised when he turned right at the mid-ship staircase when the Adriatic suite was close to the front. She passed a couple in front and caught up enough to see Barker turn left onto the staircase and head upwards. Crew members were standing in front of the lift doors to stop people using them and directing them towards the nearest muster stations. Barker skipped up the stairs two at a time, turning at each flight landing. Maria's longer stride meant she was almost caught up with him now.

"John, where are you going?" Maria said

Barker pretended he didn't hear her and went up to Deck Seven, turning right out of the staircase and right again down a corridor full of staterooms and worried passengers. Maria followed and caught up to him. In a gap between people, she said, 'We're on the wrong level John.'

"I'm going over the top," Barker replied without turning around. "Too risky to go straight there, past that door."

Maria smiled politely at a family coming the other way and

didn't respond. Barker turned right again at the forward staircase but was stopped by a crew member wearing a life jacket.

"Which muster station do you need sir?"

"Er..." Barker started,

"What's your room number?" said the crew member, trying to be helpful.

Barker thought quickly. They needed to go down so he made up a number beginning with 6 and hoped for the best.

"6420," he said.

"OK, down here sir," said the crew member pointing to the staircase where Barker had wanted to go all along. "Your muster station is in the theatre, bottom floor."

"Thank you," said Barker as Maria caught up and linked arms with him.

"Come on darling, we need to hurry," she said, smiling apologetically at the crew member as they headed down the staircase.

Chapter 86

In the Adriatic Suite, the hostages were the only passengers who knew the real reason for the general alarm and the decision to abandon ship. After the piercing whistles had finished and they'd all stared wide-eyed at one another, Janet shouted, 'You have to let us go! We have to get our life jackets.'

Lucy wasn't so easily fooled, breathed deeply and looked directly at Michael. But the question in her mind was spoken by someone else.

"This is something to do with you isn't it?" Jordan piped up from his position sat on the floor with his back against the wall. They'd all had their blindfolds removed to make them more comfortable and were beginning to get a bit braver.

"Yes it is," replied Michael, turning away from Lucy's stare and towards Jordan. "This is me giving Miss Jones' father a bit more to think about. A lot more actually. A demonstration of intent you might say. Obviously, he doesn't care enough about her to part with his money, but I didn't come with just one plan. Now we move on to the next stage"

"Don't hurt us. Please don't hurt us. I have a child..." said Sam Smithson, Jordan's wife, desperately.

Michael turned and smiled at her then turned away without speaking and looked at Lucy. "That's out of my hands."

Chapter 87

On Deck Six, Daryl and Rose were looking through the windows to see where the noise was coming from. It was the noise of machinery whirring and clanking, accompanied by voices, instructions being shouted and confirmed. A well-oiled machine of metal and people being put into action. The bottoms of the lifeboats were just becoming visible as they began to be lowered into their loading positions at Deck Seven, the promenade deck. The sight of moving lifeboats caused a flutter of anxiety among the passengers that shared their dining-room Muster Station with them, who thought they might have missed their opportunity of rescue.

"Ladies and gentlemen, please remain calm. The lifeboats are being lowered into their loading positions. In a few moments we'll begin to take you up to Deck Seven and allow you to board them. We'll take you out section by section, so please wait for instructions from the crew member nearest to you. Thank you." The announcement came just in time and visibly calmed the group down.

Rose was chatting to a woman next to her at the unlaid dining table, as she usually would in a social situation, whilst Daryl was scanning the crowd and the exits to see which way he thought they were likely to be taken out and up to Deck

Seven. They were roughly in the middle of the dining room as they hadn't been the first to arrive, so didn't get to sit nearest the exit. But the aft staircase was only a few yards beyond so it wouldn't be too long a walk and only one deck up before they were led out onto the promenade deck and the safety of the lifeboat. He remembered he hadn't put sunscreen on yet and wondered if there was a small bottle in his day pack on his knee. They might be stood on deck for ages and he was prone to burning. He noticed people in wheelchairs and on frames were already beyond the exit doors and were presumably being taken to the lifts. Once they were out of the way, the rest of them could go.

A crew member walked over to the table nearest the exit and said, "OK folks, if these six tables could stand up and follow me please." He waved his arms at a group of tables and passengers just beyond them looked at each other hopefully. Daryl knew they would have been in that group if they'd arrived earlier. He watched the first sixty people shuffle towards the exit door and touched his wife's arm reassuringly and nodded towards the door.

On the opposite side of the room the same was happening with the first group of tables, only they were being led out of the exit on that side and up to lifeboats on the port side of the ship. How would they split people in the centre of the room, Daryl wondered, and was glad they'd sat clearly on one side. His greatest worry about cruising was being split from his wife. He worried when they were in port and she wandered off into a shop and he momentarily couldn't see her. Irrationally, he worried they might not both make it back to the ship, even though they were well travelled and Rose was quite capable of looking after herself. He breathed in and out and relaxed at the thought they were going to leave the ship together.

All over the ship, in all the other Muster Stations, crew-members were shepherding passengers slowly towards the exits and onto the promenade deck and their waiting lifeboats. It was the first time most of the crew had done this for real and they were excited and a little scared, but their training was thorough and professional. They were helped by ideal weather and a calm sea. It could have been worse. A lot worse.

Chapter 88

On Deck Five Barker and Maria turned right out of the staircase and right again into the port side corridor that led to the Adriatic suite, but continued walking past the lobby area where the entrance was, pretending to be heading for their stateroom to pick up their life-jackets. There were still a few people about, life jackets in hand, heading quickly in the other direction, late for their muster stations.

Barker was nervous now as he knew, or at least suspected, that Lucy was still in the room they were walking past. Why didn't he just barge in and rescue her? That's what he felt he ought to do. He felt physically inadequate at the thought he couldn't protect her. But he'd never been that kind of cop. Besides, he might only get one chance and he couldn't mess it up. So they walked past into the Sanctuary, a part of the spa where guests go to chill before or after their treatments. It was a lounge area with a dozen or so sets of tables and chairs, and a similar amount of small sofas with coffee tables between. The far wall was tinted glass, and through it they could see the therapy pool, a small, extravagantly-decorated room with a chest-deep pool only just big enough for a dozen or so people. There was a waterfall feature behind it and metal spouts pointing down with jets of water firing into the pool, usually after bouncing off the bodies of the well-heeled guests who'd paid the extra charge to use it. The tables and chairs were not arranged neatly and there were cups and plates left lying around after the staff had left in a hurry.

As they turned right into the room, on their right side was a small counter and kitchen behind, backing onto the Adriatic suite. Barker ignored the mess and walked straight round the end of the counter and into the tiny kitchen area. He was surprised how small it was but realised it wasn't the busiest place on the ship, perhaps serving just a few dozen people a day, those that could afford the massages and facials and fancy electro therapies on offer. He'd looked at the menu of treatments available in his stateroom, and quickly put it down again.

The kitchen was all stainless steel tables and preparation surfaces and cupboards, with a few small appliances for cooking the few hot meals on offer. Salad, vegetables and breads were lying partially-sliced on the surfaces, abandoned like the tables outside when the alarm had sounded. Barker scanned the back wall and in the stainless steel sheet on the wall there was a door with a steel handle which he quickly walked over to and pushed down. In his haste he didn't realise that he might have walked straight into the suite, unprepared for what he might find. Luckily, he found himself in a dry storeroom with racks of metal shelving stuffed with ingredients. The room was half the size of the kitchen and lined with white plastic panels. On the far wall about eight feet away was another door.

Chapter 89

Most of the ship by now was quite empty. Crew-members stood dutifully by lifts and staircases and doorways to make sure confused passengers couldn't get lost. Others walked to-and-fro looking for strays and checking off lists.

Deck Seven meanwhile was full of queues of passengers snaking out of their muster stations, along corridors and out onto the promenade deck, which was a heaving mass of bodies patiently waiting their turn to board a lifeboat and get to safety. The sun beat down but there was a gentle breeze and the overhanging structure of the ship and its lifeboat supports was casting enough shadow to protect people from sunburn. The sea was calm, inviting even, and the sight of land on the horizon kept most people from panicking.

The first lifeboat on the starboard side was full and the door clunked shut by an engineer who checked the locking handles before a reassuringly smooth and solid whirring began as the boat slowly lowered downwards below the handrail and out of sight. A ripple of excitement ran through the crowd as they understood that they were on their way.

Daryl and Rose were in a queue that was just coming out through a door onto the aft end of the promenade deck on the starboard side. They could just see over the heads of those in front of them the sight of the first lifeboat leaving. The boat they were queueing for was about fifteen yards ahead of them, the second to last along that side of the ship. There were about forty to fifty people in the queue ahead of them and loading was slowing down. Daryl wondered if they were going to make it on or would have to wait and move forward to the next one, probably twenty minutes queueing away.

As he stepped out through the door into the fresh air he looked around and saw a webbing barrier stretched between two posts across the deck, preventing access to the rearmost lifeboat which stood empty. Grabbing his wife's hand he said, 'Come on Rose,' and pulled her out of the queue and round the side of the post and back down the deck towards the empty boat.

"No Daryl, we should wait," said Rose

"It's empty. Come on." Daryl replied, guiding Rose up the steps and down into the fibreglass hull of the empty boat. "Better to be on one early and find a seat than get stuck standing up and crammed in by a doorway. It'll fill up soon."

A few people in the queue alongside them looked at the empty boat but didn't follow. One of them mentioned what had happened to the crew-member guiding them to the nearly-full boat in front of them, but he was unable to leave his post. Another two lifeboats further forward began to clunk and whirr and lower down below into the Caribbean Sea. As did Daryl and Rose's.

Chapter 90

Aidan Jones walked through the door into his office building for the second time this morning and took off his coat. He'd been down to the car park and sat in his royal blue Bentley Continental for five minutes deciding whether to drive off and hide away somewhere quiet for a few days. Somewhere they couldn't find him. He had the resources and the contacts, and enough favours to call in. But it would only delay the inevitable. They would find him eventually.

They found him in reception. As Aidan smiled at Jodie on the front desk for the second time this morning, he felt someone grab his left shoulder, spin him around and push him back against the reception desk. Jodie gasped, jumped up and stepped back from her seat.

"Tell me what you did Aidan. Tell me everything," said Stephen Mitchell, grabbing a fist full of Aidan's tailored white shirt.

"I'm calling the police," said Jodie picking up the receiver on the desk's handset.

"No Jodie, don't," said Aidan, "It's OK. Stephen's upset. We'll go into the conference room as soon as he puts me down, won't we Stephen?"

Stephen stared into Aidan's eyes hard and his face squirmed

with anger. His skin was blotchy red. He pushed Aidan back again and let go of his shirt but kept his eyes on him in case he made a run for the door. Aidan stood up off the desk and straightened his shirt collar and jacket.

"This way," he said as he turned into the downstairs corridor and pushed open the first door on his right into the board room. Reluctantly Stephen followed as a car screeched into the car park and came to an abrupt halt in front of the main door. Two middle-aged women stepped out.

Helen Gibson and Diane Collins pushed through the door and caught sight of the back of Stephen following Aidan through a door. Jodie mouthed a greeting at them but was ignored as the two women marched down the corridor and into the conference room.

Inside the room, Aidan had walked around the central table to try to put an obstacle between him and Stephen, but Stephen followed him. He looked over Stephen's shoulder as Diane and Helen appeared and stood by the door as if to make sure he couldn't leave easily.

"Sit down," Diane said, through gritted teeth, "And explain why five people have died on your ship, and why eight others are being held hostage."

Aidan grabbed the nearest chair and slid down into it. One by one the others did the same, none of them taking their eyes off him.

"The truth Aidan," Helen added. "We've had a version of it in the email we've all received this morning. What you tell us now needs to match that or we just call the police."

Aidan looked down at the table, breathed deeply and considered his options. He could make up whatever story he wanted and they wouldn't know any different. But whatever that email said was likely to be loosely based on what had actually happened, even if it was coming from one man's biased viewpoint. So he decided to give them his.

"I set up a deal." Aidan began.

"A drug deal." Diane interrupted, glaring at him.

"A deal. It doesn't really matter what kind of deal."

"Of course it matters Aidan, because when drug deals go wrong they tend to have consequences, and not just financial ones. So don't give me that crap."

"It didn't go wrong. Not for me anyway…"

"It's gone wrong now!" shouted Stephen, sat next to Aidan on his left side.

Aidan took a breath and continued. "One of the idiots involved at the other end got caught. He's pissed off and taking it out on me."

"Why would he do that?" Diane asked, "Why is he mad at you?"

"Because half of the…consignment was for him. He screwed up, I ended up with almost all of it and he got nothing."

"How did he screw up?" Helen asked.

"They were tipped off that the coastguard was coming and went to Plan B – a smaller, faster boat that could take the cargo and get away and take him with it. Most of it had been transferred when the small boat captain decided to leave. He should have been on it but was still on the mother ship. His fault, not mine. He went down for five years."

"So you sold the goods and made your money while he was in prison?" Stephen asked.

After a pause, Aidan nodded.

"Why didn't you keep his half for him?" Helen asked.

"You can't keep stuff like that hanging around while somebody's away for a few years. It has to be moved on."

"You could've saved his share of the money and given it to him later," said Helen.

"I think that's what's happening now," said Aidan, trying not to sound sarcastic.

"See? Consequences," Diane said, "It couldn't be electronics or cosmetics or clothes? How often have you done this Aidan?"

"Sorry Diane, I don't care what he's done before," Stephen said, "We need to know what he's going to do now. Right now. About these people."

Stephen pulled his cell phone out of his pocket and scrolled to the photo attached to the email they'd all received earlier that morning. A photo of seven or eight people sat on the floor of a room with their hands tied behind them, some gagged and/or blindfolded. Aidan didn't recognise them.

Except for Lucy.

Aidan took a deep breath when saw his daughter. "I don't negotiate with terrorists. Our government wouldn't so why should I?"

Chapter 91

"Don't John," said Maria quietly as she followed him into the food store and saw him looking intently at the door in the back wall. The door had a twist lock on it in place of a handle, meaning it was lockable from this side, presumable for when plates of food were carried through for events in the suite itself.

Barker looked around at her blankly.

"Not yet," she said, shaking her head. "We need to find out what's going on in there first. Try that," she said, pointing down at a vent in the wall to the left of the door.

Barker looked down at the silver metal louvre vent and scanned around the wall for others. There was one at the top of the wall directly above. He got down on his knees and looked into the slats but all he could see was carpet directly below on the other side. Putting his ear to it instead he could hear movement of chairs or tables and people mumbling. He sat back and stood up and looked at the vent higher up, then scanned the room for something to stand on. Maria looked around too and found a large box of tinned tomatoes. Barker grabbed it and found another and stacked them up before standing on them. His head was brushing the ceiling but he was at the perfect height to look through the vent. He still couldn't see straight through but could just about see across the bottom half of the room: carpet, chairs, a table, people's legs, and on the right-hand side of the room, half a dozen people sat on the floor leaning against the wall with their hands tied behind their backs.

"And?" whispered Maria.

"Shhhh,' Barker replied putting his finger to his lips as he looked at her, "They're in there," He whispered before stepping down off the boxes.

"Who is? Who can you see?"

"I don't know. I can't see the whole room. Some of the people we had in there yesterday are sat on the floor along the far wall. I recognise a couple, but there are others I don't. There are a few people stood up around a table by the door and someone sat on a chair."

"Lucy?"

"Can't see her."

"She may not even be in there John. This could be a trap. Did you check her stateroom?"

Barker looked at her embarrassed, "No. I..."

A voice drifted through the vent more clearly. A voice that Maria knew well.

Chapter 92

Rose was upset with Daryl and tried to get up from her seat just in front of the door in the centre of the side of the lifeboat as it got nearer to the sea below, but Daryl held her back.

"Sit down Rose," said Daryl.

"We've got to get off!" Rose replied.

"We can't, we're moving now."

"They've made a mistake. *We've* made a mistake. We shouldn't be on here."

"It doesn't matter Rose. We're in a lifeboat. We're safe. We're going to be fine."

"They'll pull us back up."

"That's OK," said Daryl. "Then they'll realise their mistake and fill us up with more people. And we'll come back down again. Either way we're OK."

"I want to go home."

"We're going home Rose. Just as soon as we hit the sea, we'll be off to the shore and then they'll arrange flights for us all to get back home."

"We're supposed to be in Florida."

"I know. Well maybe they'll send us there first. Maybe they'll fix the ship and put us back on it and send us on our way. We've another day to go yet."

Rose sat back down and held Daryl's hand. She looked out of one of the tiny portholes that serve as windows in the tiny plastic-hulled boat.

Chapter 93

"Aidan. Me again," said Michael into his cell phone, stood in front of the table by the door in the Adriatic suite, a couple of feet in front of Lucy's chair. "Have they arrived yet?"

"Have who arrived?" Came the reply.

"Don't mess about Aidan. You don't have the time. The board. Some, if not all of them?"

"Some, yes."

"What do they think?"

"Depends on your point of view."

"Sounds promising. What about the money."

"Nope."

"Are you sure? Last chance Aidan. Have you even told them?"

"Not happening."

Michael paused for effect.

"Then I have something that will hopefully change your minds."

Michael nodded at a man in a white uniform stood by the door. The man tapped his cell phone and spoke a few words in Spanish into it. He looked down at his screen for a few seconds and handed the phone to Michael. Michael looked at the video playing on the screen for a few seconds and saw a lifeboat being lowered off the starboard side of the ship. He tapped at the screen and then spoke again into his own cell phone.

"Aidan. Look at your company's Facebook page. I've just shared a link of what's happening over here. I think you need to see it. Show it to the others."

In the conference room Aidan looked around the table at the other faces staring back at him waiting for him to tell them what was going on. A cell phone pinged to indicate a text message received. Helen scrabbled in her handbag and pulled out her new Samsung. She looked up at Stephen and Aidan and down again at her phone.

"'Just in case he doesn't show you,'" she read out aloud, "There's a link."

"Tap it," said Diane, sat on Helen's right-hand side. "Is that working?" pointing at the large LCD screen at the end of the room.

Stephen stood up and switched the screen on. Helen tapped her cell phone screen and waited for the link to open. Diane took the phone from her and tapped some more. The screen flickered into life for a couple of seconds and then the video that was playing on the cell phone in Michael's right-hand onboard Starlight was also playing on Helen's phone screen and the big screen in the conference room. It showed an orange lifebelt fastened to the ship's handrail. The lettering arcing around the top spelled out 'GALAXY', and around the bottom, 'STARLIGHT'. Whoever was holding the camera then moved forward and pointed it at the sea where the first lifeboats were heading for the shore, before swinging around and zooming in on one particular little boat.

"Just in case you doubted me," said Michael into Aidan's

267

ear. Aidan jumped at the words now that his attention was entirely on the big screen in front of them all. He said nothing.

Lucy began to get agitated. It was clear something bad was happening and she didn't know what.

"What are you doing Michael? What's going on?"

"I'm showing your father that he needs to take me more seriously."

"By doing what?"

"You'll know in a minute. You'll hear it."

"Hear it?"

Daryl and Rose's lifeboat stopped lowering and bounced gently down onto the surface of the water below. Almost immediately an engine started and the wire ropes that had lowered them down clanked away and raised up out of the way. A gearbox engaged with the engine and the little orange boat began to reverse back past Starlight's stern. Once clear, the boat swung around, paused, and headed forwards away from the cruise ship.

"We're going the wrong way!" Rose cried out, spinning around looking through the small windows.

"Calm down Rose," said Daryl, "We'll swing round once we're clear."

Footsteps clunked around the rear corner of the boat.

"The driver. I'd forgotten about the driver," said Daryl, standing up and staggering towards the back of the boat to see if he could see where the driver was sat at the back in a small seat above the passengers with his head poking up outside so he could guide the boat along.

"He's not there. There's no one there."

Chapter 94

"That's him, that's Michael. I can't make out what he's saying," whispered Maria, crouching on the floor to get her head near to the lower vent.

"I think he's on the phone."

"Who to? What's he saying?"

"Lots of questions. Something about money. Who's Aidan?"

"I don't know."

A deep, dull boom rattled the shelves in the storeroom. It came from the opposite end of the ship, off to Barker's left. The starboard side probably. It was strong enough to make him steady himself on the boxes.

"What was that?" said Barker.

Maria looked up at him and said, "Shh, keep listening."

"More voices. I can hear more people. The hostages. They're upset. Whatever that was, it wasn't good."

"None of this is good John."

Stephen Mitchell visibly recoiled when he heard the noise and watched the lifeboat explode on the conference room screen. Helen Gibson gasped out loud and Diane covered her mouth with her hand. Aidan's face went white. Nobody spoke while they watched the shards of debris raining down on the

Caribbean sea. Nothing recognisable remained. Diane turned and stared at Aidan. Aidan looked at her open-mouthed.

"Changed your mind yet?" Came a voice through Aidan's cell phone.

Aidan put his phone to his left ear but still couldn't speak.

"I take it you saw that?" said Michael.

"Yes," Aidan replied.

"And?"

"How many people were on that?"

"Not important. What's important is that you understand we have enough explosive left to put a hole in the side of Starlight and send it to the bottom of the sea. It's quite shallow here. It might even stick up above the waves as a permanent reminder."

"Michael, don't..."

"No more discussion Aidan. Twenty million wired to my bank in the next ten minutes. Set it up. Then I'll put the account details in from here. I'll put you on to my IT guy."

"Twenty? Your share was ten!"

"The cost of broken promises Aidan. Twenty or your daughter's next."

Michael passed the phone to one of the men stood by a laptop on the table behind him.

Chapter 95

Barker stepped down off the boxes and sat on them. Maria stood up and turned towards him.

"He wants a ransom or he'll blow the ship," he said, looking up at her, "We have to stop him Maria."

Maria nodded. "What's the layout of the room?"

From memory Barker replied, "About forty feet square. Can't see anyone at this end. All the chairs from yesterday have gone. They might be stacked up against the wall at this end. Michael is stood this side of a table where the laptop is, but at the far end of the room. There are a few people stood around it, presumably his cronies. The hostages are sat on the floor with their backs against the far wall. There's someone sitting on a chair sideways on to the table. I think that's Lucy."

"How can you tell?"

"I can't really. But it's definitely a female."

Maria thought for a few seconds, "So we go in through this door. I'll walk in, to the right, and surprise Michael. You run round to the left and grab Lucy."

"What, just like that?"

"Michael will crap himself when he sees me. Besides, this will help."

Maria reached around her back and pulled a small pistol

from the waistband of her jeans.

"Jesus. When were you going to tell me about that?" said Barker.

"About now," Maria replied.

Barker looked at Maria, breathed deeply and said, "We can't afford to mess this up."

"I have no intention of messing it up." She replied.

Barker climbed back up on the boxes to take a last look. "Looks the same," he said, "No-one's moved much. You'll have to twist that lock and go through in one movement. I'll jump down and follow as soon as you go."

Maria looked up at him and nodded, then turned to look down at the silver metal latch between the fingers of her right hand. Her right shoulder was pressed gently against the door ready to push it open, and the pistol was in her left hand. She took a deep breath, then another, and twisted the lock.

Chapter 96

Michael's IT guy stepped back from the laptop and gestured toward it, 'It's ready. He's logged in. He's setting up the payment.'

"Good," said Michael, "Where do I put the number in?"

IT guy leaned over again and pointed to boxes on the screen where Michael would enter his bank details.

"I suppose it's nice to know he's got some standards, even if he doesn't care about me,' said Lucy, still sat on the chair in front of the table."

Michael, happy with the IT guy's instructions, turned to Lucy, "I guess you were right Lucy, he doesn't give a..." he stopped mid-sentence and jumped back, when a door in the wall opposite him swung open and slammed back on its hinges. A woman launched herself through the opening towards him, starting low and straightening up as she got to the middle of the room, with her left arm out holding a weapon. A couple of Michael's crew moved to pick up their own guns in slow motion.

As soon as Barker saw Maria shoulder the door open he jumped off the boxes, landed behind her and prepared to run to the left and round to grab Lucy. But something was up. It wasn't going how he'd visualised it. Maria said she would stop in the middle of the room, to the right, and let him run past. But she hadn't stopped. She'd carried on directly towards Lucy, pointing the pistol at Michael standing behind Lucy and grabbing her around the neck. Barker found himself stopped in the middle of the room with nowhere to go and no weapon.

"John?" shouted Lucy.

Barker glanced at Lucy with a brief relief, then up at Maria. His arms went out to the sides, palms up,

"What...?" he said, staring at Maria.

Two people stood by the hostages pointed their weapons at Maria and started screaming "Put it down! Put it down!"

Maria turned the pistol and pressed it against Lucy's left temple and stared back at the guards. Then she looked at Michael.

"Surprise," she said calmly.

Michael was rooted to the spot in front of the laptop table, staring at Maria in disbelief.

"I...Maria, I..."

"Didn't expect to see me did you?"

"What the hell Maria? Why...?" shouted Barker from the middle of the room.

"Shut up now John..." Maria said, twisting to the right, still holding Lucy. Lucy groaned. "You couldn't keep your nose out John, so I had to bring you with me, keep you close."

Maria turned to look at Michael again. "No time to explain Michael. Change of plan. Call your men off, him included. Weapons on the table," nodding at the IT guy stood at the end of the desk.

Michael turned and nodded to the IT guy and guards behind. They stepped forwards, placed their guns on the desk while not taking their eyes off Maria. Then they took a few steps backwards towards the hostages.

Barker looked at Lucy, shrugged, and shook his head. He'd been so close, but he'd been a fool. He should have gone in by himself and never trusted Maria.

"You tried to have me killed Michael."

"What did you expect?"

"I expected to help you. To look after our home until you came back."

"They would have got to you sooner or later. You would have helped them. They would have found out about everything. Not just that one shipment. I had no choice."

"Well now you have no choice. That money is as much mine as it is yours. I worked hard for you. For us. We had a life. You tried to take my life but I survived. And then I had to hide. My world changed. And my son. Our son..."

Lucy wriggled as Maria pressed the barrel harder into the side of her head.

"I'm going to give you a different account number to enter into that box Michael, *my* account number."

Michael stiffened and said, "It's not your money."

"I hold the cards now Michael. You've screwed this up for the second time. Accept it and we all live to see another day."

Maria pulled the pistol away from the side of Lucy's head and pointed it at Michael, loosening her grip slightly around Lucy's neck. She ordered Michael to enter the numbers and turn the laptop to face her so she could confirm.

"Enter it," Maria said.

Chapter 97

Barker was staring at the confrontation between Maria and Michael when he noticed in his peripheral vision Lucy's right hand moving. Her hands were still untied from when she called her father and Maria hadn't noticed. Her fingers seemed to move randomly but then Barker understood what she was doing. She pointed her thumb at herself, then her first finger upwards towards Maria. Then she pointed at Barker, and then at Michael. Barker looked up at Lucy's face and saw her eyes widen and her lips mouth the word "Now."

In the space of a couple of seconds, Barker looked up to assess the chance of Lucy's plan working. Maria was pointing her pistol at Michael, basking in the glow of inflating her bank account by twenty million dollars. Michael had the exact opposite feeling. He was losing it again and his 'dead' wife had stolen it from him. His attention was on the keyboard. The guards were distracted watching this unfold and not interested in Barker who was unarmed. No one was looking at him, except Lucy and, it turned out, a couple of the hostages who seemed to be thinking what he was thinking.

This was it, one of those fortuitous moments when things coalesce in your favour, but it would only last a split second more if he was lucky. He had to act now if there was any chance of success. He dropped almost to a crouch, tipped his weight towards the entrance door and launched himself in a sprint towards Michael. He was there in three or four strides and too fast for anyone to stop him.

Lucy watched Barker intensely and as soon as he began to move she stood bolt upright and tipped her head back, cracking underneath Maria's jaw and sending her helplessly backwards onto the floor.

Barker hit Michael with his left shoulder just above waist height and momentum took both of them crashing into and over the table, sending the laptop smashing onto the floor.

Maria landed heavily and banged the back of her head on the floor but, realising she'd lost control of the situation, fired at random across the room, hitting one of Michael's guards, who were both by now starting to move towards her and Barker. The guard fell face-first onto the floor halfway across the room and rolled over onto his back, grabbing his shoulder where he'd been hit.

Lucy bent forwards and tipped her chair upwards and backwards, sliding its legs out of the tie-wraps that had been holding her to it and darted for the entrance door, making a grab for Barker's shirt as he tried to get up.

As he stood up and jumped out of Michael's way, Barker watched Lucy push the door open and go through it. Lucy pulled him through and said, "This way. Run!"

Chapter 98

Diane Collins couldn't hold back the tears. Helen held her face in her hands and Stephen Mitchell stood up behind Aidan who was tapping at a laptop on the board room table, his face going grey. He looked like a man who was about to lose twenty million dollars. With every keystroke he wondered how he could avoid the inevitable. Either way he would lose. Either twenty million or his daughter. But that decision wasn't the hard one. They had fallen out many times and he hadn't seen her for years. He didn't even know where she was working. It wasn't her fault if she'd found herself in the wrong place at the wrong time.

No, the decision was twenty million or Starlight. If Michael wasn't bluffing and put a hole in his flagship and sent it to the seabed he would lose a lot more than twenty million. Insurers would probe too deeply and he didn't need that. If that happened and the truth came out he'd go down for years. Better to get out with a little than lose everything.

"What's happening?" Stephen asked.

"I don't know, he's taking his time giving me his account details," Aidan replied. "I'm not in a hurry."

"The sooner you get this done, the sooner we get this finished."

"Finished?"

"You're not walking out of here and going back to your normal life Aidan. People have died."

"I've not killed anybody!" Aidan shouted.

"They died because of what you started Aidan," said Stephen, leaning over Aidan's left shoulder and breathing down his neck. "I can't do anything about the other guy. But I can sort you out."

Stephen Mitchell was taller than Aidan and had been an athlete in his younger days. For the first time, Aidan realised he might not get out of the building on his own terms and began to sweat.

Chapter 99

Lucy ran barefoot down the port-side corridor towards the mid-ships staircase. Barker followed noticing soreness in his chest and thigh where he'd fallen onto the table, but now wasn't the time to think about that. His legs were working as well as they ever did so he just about kept up with Lucy, who turned left at the staircase and immediate right up one flight of stairs, turning left again down the stateroom corridor. After a few strides she darted left into a doorway. Barker noticed the *Launderette* sign above it.

Inside, Lucy stood in the middle of the narrow room, which stretched across from port to starboard corridors. There were four washing machines, three dryers and four ironing boards along one side of the room. Barker burst through the door gasping for air and slowed down as he walked over to Lucy. Lucy put her arms around his shoulders and hugged him tight for a couple of seconds, then pulled back, looked him in the eye and pressed her lips against his for another couple of seconds. They separated and looked at one another, but before either could say anything the door burst open.

Lucy jumped back and Barker span around to see who it was. At first he didn't recognise the face and was ready to run again.

"We followed you. We saw you come in," said Jordan,

breathlessly, his wife Sam following him into the room. "We got out. It was chaos in there. I don't know about the others." The door opened again seconds later and in walked a face Barker *did* recognise.

"Marcus?!" said Barker. Marcus just nodded and leaned forward putting his hands on his knees and gasped for air, eventually turning to put his back against the wall and slumping down onto the floor.

"What now?" Jordan said, "We can't stay here. They'll come after us."

"Did they follow you?" Barker asked.

"No. Pretty sure. There was shouting but I think there was too much going on in there. But this isn't a good place to hide."

"No," said Barker, thinking for a moment and turning to Lucy. "What's your date of birth?"

"What?"

"Birthday. Day and month."

"Er...twenty-first of August. Why?"

"Twenty-one, eight. Two, one, eight. Is there a room two-one-eight on this floor?"

"Er, yeah, I think so."

"Floors above?"

"Probably."

"OK, go one floor up and find room 218. Take this." Barker reached round to his back pocket and pulled out the master Sea Star they'd used to get into the Gibson and Mitchell rooms. "It should let you in. Take Sam and Jordan with you."

Lucy took the disc off him, "Quick thinking. You're on form today." Then she frowned, "What about you?"

"I need a word with Marcus. Wait there for me. I won't be long. If you have to move, just go up a deck to another 218.

I'll find you. If you need to escape, climb out over the balcony. Quick, Go."

Lucy motioned at Jordan and Sam to follow her out through the starboard side door. Barker turned the locks on the inside of both doors and sat down next to Marcus.

Chapter 100

In the Adriatic Suite, Maria picked herself up off the floor and stood up, still pointing her weapon in the direction of Michael's guards. The second one stopped in his tracks after her wild shot had downed his colleague, and he put his hands in the air in front of him.

"Lie down," said Maria, "Face down. Next to your friend."

The man did as he was told, getting to his knees and lying prostrate on the floor, avoiding the blood coming out of his friend's shoulder, who was lying on his back gasping for air.

"He'll live," said Maria, keeping the gun trained on them both.

By the door, Michael groaned and tried to get up from the floor where he'd fallen. Maria span round to her left and waved the gun at him.

"Think about it Michael. Don't be stupid."

Michael groaned again, rubbing the back of his head where it had hit the wall, as he sat up.

"You! Over there. Yes, you." Maria nodded across the room at Jasmine who had backed up to the wall during the commotion and kept out of trouble.

"Me?" said Jasmine, looking hopefully to either side to see if Maria meant someone else.

"Yes, you. You can help. Pick up the rest of those cable-ties and tie his hands before he gets up," said Maria, "And don't put up a fight Michael."

Jasmine obediently walked over to the upturned table, bent down and picked up a couple of cable-ties, and shuffled around to where Michael sat. She squatted next to him and waved the tie at his wrists to indicate that he should put them together in front of his body, then proceeded to wrap one around and click one end through the other and pull it tight.

"Careful!" Michael winced.

"Another one. Then the same with these two, hands and feet," said Maria, gesturing at the guards on the floor. "Then tie their feet to each other. I don't want them going anywhere."

Jasmine continued carefully, and Maria allowed herself to take a deep breath in relative safety. She looked across to the wall opposite where a few of the hostages were still cowering.

"I'm not here to harm you, but I need you to co-operate for a while longer. In a few minutes, we'll be leaving. But you will be staying here until we've left the ship. If I see you outside this room I will shoot you."

"Done", confirmed Jasmine, standing upright and looking at Maria with a deadpan stare.

"Good. Pick up that laptop. Is it still working?"

Jasmine moved back around the table and picked up the device.

"It's from engineering, so it's more robust than average. It'll be fine," said Michael.

"Lucky for you. Wouldn't want to drag this out for much longer. The sooner I don't have to see your face anymore the better."

"Ditto." mumbled Michael, "What's your next move?"

Maria shrugged, "Once I'm done here I'm going to take you with me and throw you overboard. If you behave yourself I'll throw a life-jacket in after you. Then I'm going to leave."

"It's OK. It's still on the same page," Jasmine said as she placed the laptop onto the chair and turned it around so Maria could see it."

"It still has the account number I entered in the box?"

"Yes."

"Press Enter."

Jasmine hit the Enter button and Maria breathed in a deep breath of satisfaction and looked at Michael, who looked away.

"It's timed out," said Jasmine.

"What?" Maria replied.

"It's timed out. Because nobody's touched it for a few minutes."

"Shit. Log back in," Maria said, looking at Michael and waving the gun again.

Michael flashed Maria a hard stare and struggled to his feet, unable to support himself properly with his tied hands. He stumbled around the table to the chair and leaned over it, touching the trackpad to refresh the page and enter the login details he'd been given by Aidan.

"Happy?" he said.

"Not yet. Move over there with the others. Face the wall."

"Seriously?"

"What do *you* think?"

Michael shuffled backwards to the wall next to the hostages and turned around to face it. The door was only six feet away. He could make a run for it but he knew Maria was watching. He could feel her eyes in the back of his head. And she'd already used her gun. He'd taught her how to use one. For self defence at home.

"Enter these numbers," Maria said to Jasmine, giving her the account number she'd forced Michael to enter before. "Now back off."

Jasmine backed up as Maria walked up to the laptop to check the details.

"Good," she said as she backed away, "Now hit Enter again."

Jasmine did as she was told and the screen asked for confirmation. She looked up at Maria.

"And again," said Maria.

Jasmine hit the key in the hope it was the last time and she would be allowed to go and join the others along the wall and be out of danger. She looked up at Maria again and saw a broad grin forming on her face.

"Thank you. Now you can come with us. Stand by the door facing away from me."

Jasmine looked crestfallen but turned to walk to the door.

"Michael? You stand behind her. The three of us are going to leave now. If either of you runs I will shoot you both."

Chapter 101

Aidan felt the blood drain from his face as he watched the live balance of his private account reduce by twenty million dollars. So far he'd hoped it wasn't really happening, that something would stop it all. But now he had to go into survival mode. His instincts had to kick in and he had to protect himself and get out with as much as he possibly could, even if that was just the Bentley sat in the car park.

"Helen, would you ring the police please?" Stephen asked. "Somebody needs to come and deal with him. And tell them what happened to the lifeboat. I'm sure the authorities over there know by now, but it will help put the puzzle together if we tell them what we know."

Just as Stephen finished speaking, Aidan stood up and rammed the metal frame off his chair backwards into Stephen's shins, and scrambled onto and across the conference table towards Diane and Helen on the opposite side by the door. Stephen yelled in pain and stumbled back against a windowsill before regaining his balance and starting to move around the top end of the table.

But Aidan was too far ahead. Diane recoiled out of his way and Helen, already dialling, stepped back and shouted "Police! Please, quickly!"

Aidan swung the door open and slipped through it, turned left into the corridor and burst through reception and out into the car park. He patted his right trouser pocket to see if he still had his car keys with him. At this point, something so simple could be life-changing. Stephen burst through the entrance door about five metres behind Aidan but slipped on the wet tarmac, falling on his face in the rain. He was up again in a second or two, but it was enough to allow Aidan time to open his car door, jump inside and press the button that locked the doors.

"Get out you bastard!" Stephen shouted as he reached the front of the car, putting his hands on the hood.

Aidan prodded the starter button before taking a couple of quick, deep breaths. Stephen was hammering on the bodywork with his fists and feet, but Aidan didn't care. He saw Helen walking out of the door behind Stephen as he slowly nudged the car forward, pushing Stephen backwards. At first he thought he was going to jump on the car and try to stop him from driving away, but Stephen knew that wasn't going to work. The last thing Aidan saw as he swung the car out of the car park was Helen filming him with her phone. He couldn't resist raising his middle finger as the tyres squealed and launched him out onto the road.

Chapter 102

Inside room 7218 on Deck Seven, Lucy opened the mini-bar and threw the contents onto the king-size bed next to where Jordan and Sam were sat. She picked up a miniature bottle of vodka and sat down in a tub chair next to the balcony doors.

"Help yourselves, I think we need it."

Sam picked up a small bottle of gin, unscrewed the cap, took a swig, and passed it to Jordan. Jordan stood up and picked a glass up off the shelf above the mini-bar and tipped the gin into it, reaching for a can of tonic water to add to it.

"What now? Where's your friend gone?" said Sam.

"I don't know," said Lucy in between sips from the small bottle, "but I trust him. He won't be long. We're fairly safe here if we don't go out again. Did you deadlock the door?"

"No," said Jordan, standing up and walking over to the door, and twisting the lock once more to the left. "Done."

Lucy stood up and pulled back the full-height net curtain across the siding glass doors to the balcony. She slowly but firmly grabbed the handle, turned it anti-clockwise, and slid the heavy door to her left just enough for her to squeeze out through it. As she did so, she became aware that she might be visible from either side if she stepped any further forward. The solid partitions gave privacy until you stood right at the handrail looking over the side, which most people would normally do. But then you can be seen by other passengers, or kidnappers, looking down the side of the ship.

She stood still and looked out over the Caribbean sea, with land on the horizon and a dozen or more white and orange plastic boats chugging hopefully towards it. She could just about make out a small flotilla of boats coming from the land out towards Starlight, in case there was anyone left on board. There was some debris floating off to one side not far from the ship, and a dozen or so inflatable lifeboats bobbing around without engines, waiting for help to arrive.

A tap on her shoulder made Lucy jump out of her daydream.

"Lucy, there's a knock at the door. It might be John but can you check? You know him better than I do," said Jordan.

Lucy walked back through the balcony door, around the bed, and up to the spyglass in the stateroom door. Sure enough, Barker was stood outside, looking nervously from side to side to see if he had been noticed. Lucy opened the door quickly, stood back, and let him in. They stood face-to-face for a split second, both wishing they were alone. Barker then turned and walked into the room next to Sam and Jordan. Lucy followed and grabbed a miniature bottle of brandy and gave it to Barker, who smiled and opened it.

"I don't think anyone saw me," he said after gulping down half the bottle.

"Where's Marcus?" said Sam.

"Doing me a favour," Barker replied. "He's safe."

"John we can't leave those other people in that room. They're in danger."

"We're unarmed Lucy, what can we do? And we don't know what's gone on in that room."

"I heard a gunshot," said Sam. Lucy and Barker both looked at her. "As we were running out. I don't know if anyone got hurt."

"John, we should find out."

"OK. But just us. You two stay here. There's no need for you to be in danger."

A ping from a cell phone made them all stop and look at one another.

"That was you," said Sam, pointing at Barker.

Barker patted his pockets and realised his phone was still there. He fished it out and saw that the screen was badly cracked from the fall into the table. But the text was legible, just.

Margaret Gibson – Emporium

Barker frowned then looked up at Lucy. "I thought this was you."

"It was. Not anymore though," said Lucy, smiling.

"Who...?"

"Jasmine. I slipped Margaret's Sea Star into her pocket when she picked me up off the floor. Looks like they're on the move."

"Or she's escaped," said Jordan. "She was looking pretty twitchy when it all kicked off."

"Too long a delay. They must be together," said Barker.

"They're about level with us, just a few decks below," said Lucy.

"Let's go."

"We're coming with you," said Sam.

"No. There's no point," replied Barker.

"You need us. We'll go down one side of the ship, you two go the other side."

Barker sighed, "OK. But just look for them. Don't do

291

anything unless we give you the nod OK?"

Sam and Jordan both nodded and Barker and Lucy walked to the stateroom door and opened it.

Chapter 103

Jasmine walked at the front of the line of three people out through the door of the Adriatic Suite and headed left and straight into the starboard corridor away from the front of the ship. A couple of feet behind her was Michael, hobbling from his fall, having cracked the back of his head and twisted his knee. Maria was a good three metres behind him, giving herself the chance to fire if he decided to try his luck and turn on her. She would see that happen and have a couple of seconds. Plenty of time to pull the trigger. And she would barely have to even aim.

"What are you going to do with all that money?" said Michael.

"Disappear, probably. Wouldn't you?" Maria replied.

"No, actually. I mean I'd hide the money, obviously, but I'd pretend like I'd never seen it. Hide in plain sight if you like. Disappearing makes you look guilty."

"Guilty of what? I didn't steal it. You gave it to me."

"At the wrong end of a gun. And anyway *Aidan* gave it to you. It bypassed me."

"Same thing."

"And how are you going to get away from here? By the time you get off the ship the passengers will be ashore and the coastguard will be on their way here."

"And how will they know? I don't have a big bag of money. I'm just another passenger, who missed the lifeboats. The ship isn't sinking. How do you know I'm not going to just sit here and wait to be rescued?"

Michael stopped suddenly. So did Maria.

"STOP!" Maria shouted at Jasmine who had walked a few feet further ahead. Jasmine stopped and slowly turned her head. "Move Michael."

"You haven't really thought about what you're going to do with me have you?" Michael said without turning around. You didn't imagine you'd get this far did you? You just thought you'd come and find me and scare me and see what happened. Did you even know about the money?"

Maria silently stepped forward and pressed the muzzle of the gun into the back of Michael's head. Michael flinched and straightened and felt a cold shiver all over his scalp.

Maria whispered into his ear, "Michael. This is your gun. You gave it to me in our home for me to protect myself and our children. You taught me how to use it. And you've seen me use it today. I managed to bring it through security onto this ship, which means I'm not as naive as you seem to think. I have contacts too. Don't make the mistake of thinking I'm working alone. And I will have no hesitation in shooting you in the back if you even speak again unless I tell you to. Now walk. Both of you."

Maria stood still for a gap to open up again as the other two moved ahead, into the Emporium at the end of the corridor.

"Keep straight. No messing around, no stopping. At the end of the shops go left around the Atrium."

Chapter 104

In the port side corridor on Deck Seven Barker and Lucy closed the door of room 7218, having given Sam and Jordan instructions to wait five minutes before leaving, so at least they wouldn't risk being caught together. They walked hesitantly at first but sped up as they realised they were sitting ducks in the long, straight corridor with nowhere to hide if they were spotted.

"I don't know what we're going to do if we see anyone Lucy," said Barker.

"Watch them? Distract them? Throw a chair?" replied Lucy, "I'll think of something."

"Well, we're not going to see anything walking down a corridor of staterooms."

"What's your plan?"

Barker turned sharp left into the opening for the staircases and right down the first steps.

"Down to the Atrium. They must be heading that way. Be careful now, they could be close."

After one flight of stairs they stepped out onto Deck Six and into a corridor that led around a corner into the top floor of the Atrium. Barker kept close to the walls and hugged any alcoves they passed, to keep as inconspicuous as possible. Lucy was barely a step behind him.

The ship was deserted. They'd never seen the Atrium this quiet in the daytime. The piano bar ahead of them on their right was strewn with abandoned drinks and chairs from the passengers who had left in a hurry. Barker continued around the circular Atrium until they were halfway around it and facing back the way they had come. Two large glass elevator shafts were prominent features at the opposite end, perfect for making an entrance into the busiest place on the ship on gala nights, or any other night for that matter.

"Voices!" Lucy whispered, pointing down to Deck Five. "Down there!"

Barker hunched down and crept over to the railings overlooking Deck Five. Lucy followed and crouched down alongside him. The voices faded and Barker was about to dismiss them when he noticed the cables in one of the elevator shafts moving. The lift itself came up from the deck below, stopped at Deck Five and the doors opened. Through the glass walls he could see the back of a man waiting to step out when the doors opened.

At the same moment, to the right of the elevators, a figure walked out of the end of the starboard corridor coming from the Emporium.

"Jasmine!" shouted Lucy, standing up at the railings.

Jasmine looked up at Lucy and instinctively decided to make a run for it, swerved to her right and ran across the middle of the Atrium disappearing underneath the floor Lucy was stood on. There was a shriek and a scuffle directly below. Barker looked at the lift again but the man had gone. *He must've heard the commotion and captured Jasmine.*

A sharp crack sounded from the corridor followed by breaking glass, as Michael fell into the Atrium, grasping his right arm with his left.

"My fucking arm!" yelled Michael.

"I told you not to run," Maria replied.

"I'm going to bleed to death."

"If you're lucky. Stand up. Walk over there. Move!"

Maria pointed her gun at Michael and at the same time waved it towards where Jasmine was being wrestled to her feet after being foiled in her escape attempt.

Lucy crouched down again next to Barker and looked at him apologetically, having given themselves away. Barker looked at her and cupped his ear with his hand as if to say, "Listen." They could hear muttered voices below but by now Maria and Michael had joined Jasmine and the new stranger underneath them on Deck Five and they couldn't make out what was being said.

Half a minute later the talking stopped abruptly. Lucy and Barker looked at each other and slowly began to stand up and look over the edge of the balcony railing. A click from behind them both was followed by a voice, "Stand up. Both of you, and turn around slowly."

Barker felt the blood drain from his face and he struggled as he got to his feet. Lucy got up a little quicker and helped him by grabbing his arm. They both turned to face the voice and Barker stumbled backwards and hit the railing, with Lucy trying to keep him upright. Facing them was a man pointing a gun. Barker said nothing, but just stared.

"Surprise," said the man calmly.

"Rob?" replied Barker.

Chapter 105

"What?!" said Lucy, looking at Rob, then back to Barker.

"I told you you needed to find a woman John. She's not the one I meant, but still. Good job."

"You bastard," mumbled Barker, steadying himself with his right arm on the railing behind him and Lucy still holding his left. "What have you done?" Barker was shaking with rage and looked like he was ready to launch himself at Rob.

"Steady John, don't do anything stupid and make the situation worse," Rob said, lifting the gun up to face level to make sure Barker didn't forget it was there.

"Worse, how can it get worse?! I lost my world and now you've brought me here to rub my face in it? Why?"

"Loose ends John. I have to tie up loose ends. You kept asking questions. You were supposed to let it go."

"Let it go? A policeman loses his wife and you expect him not to ask questions? If I find out you hurt..."

"I didn't hurt anyone John. But don't push me."

"So what now?" Barker said, "you're just going to kill us?"

"Ideally not John, no. We needed you here until we got the money and made plans to disappear. Then we can let you go."

"You expect me to believe that crap? We know too much. I don't trust you."

"Suit yourself John. Makes no difference to me. Go down that staircase," said Rob, nodding in the direction of the Atrium staircase in front of them.

Lucy grabbed Barker's hand and squeezed it, "You can trust me." she whispered.

They moved away from the railings and she encouraged Barker to come alongside her. Barker was like an old man, struggling to walk. His brain was too busy trying to process the last five minutes to be of any use moving his legs. Lucy got him on her right side and held his hand. She could feel John's body shaking. His face was clamped in determined anger. He looked like a man who could blow at any time, but also like a man who might not last that long.

When they reached the floor of the Atrium on Deck Five Maria, Michael and Jasmine were stood waiting. Barker stared hard at Maria, who ignored him and said, "Time to go."

Chapter 106

Outside, Starlight was almost alone again on the water and the noise levels created by evacuating nearly four thousand people had mostly died away. The lifeboats had all been lowered and were heading towards the shore. The only people remaining were those bobbing gently around in inflatable lifeboats, some of which had been thrown lines and were being towed slowly away from the ship by the last few powered craft. A growing stream of all kinds of small vessels was coming out from the port. Tourist catamarans, tenders, a few fishing boats: all were heading out to see if help was needed. The weather could not have been kinder. The sea was calm and the wind was just a gentle breeze.

One bright orange and white lifeboat appeared around Starlight's bow, moving in the opposite direction to the others, and chugged its way back towards the starboard gangway door.

Chapter 107

It wasn't easy leading four hostages through corridors, down stairs, around corners and through doorways, even with two armed people in charge. Rob walked at the back in case any of them decided to try turning around and making a run for it. Immediately in front of him were Barker and Lucy. Maria was next, with Michael and Jasmine ahead of her. At each bottleneck - a corridor corner or staircase, Maria and Rob would take turns to wait with their two hostages and let the others pass before following behind.

Barker cursed his lack of fitness and strength. He'd never been athletic but he'd let himself go since he left his job, and was not in good shape. Even so he felt he should be able to overpower one of them if he had a chance. He could barely contain his anger towards Rob and was tempted to just lash out, but had just enough control left to realise that, whilst he might be able to do some damage, he'd probably make the overall situation worse for the others even if he didn't care about himself.

Lucy kept a tight hold on Barker's hand, not for her own reassurance, but to be able to keep a check on how he was feeling and to hold him back from doing anything stupid. They'd got out of a situation in the Adriatic Suite, but then they'd had the element of surprise and the weapons weren't pointed at them. Now they were being marched at gunpoint through confined spaces to who knows where. She racked her brains to work out her options, including what to do if Barker flipped out. His hand was gripping hers tightly and he barely acknowledged her as they walked. She knew it wasn't about her. It was about Rob.

Michael was holding his shoulder and limping as he walked. He'd not had a good last hour. He was almost as angry and confused as Barker. The ex-wife he thought he'd disposed of had returned to haunt him and stolen twenty million dollars. He'd been screwed over by Savenas Seaways at the drop-off years ago, and now his plan to get it all back had been smashed at the death. He too mulled over his chances of escape on this short walk that seemed to be lasting forever. Normally he wouldn't hesitate to have a go, but the fall over the table inflicted by that that dumb cop Barker had cracked a couple of ribs, and given him a concussion, and Maria had added a bullet graze to his arm that meant he was very likely to be killed if he tried anything. But weren't they all going to end up feeding the fishes in a few minutes anyway?

In the end it was Jasmine who was first to react.

Rob, Lucy and Barker rounded the final corner before the gangway on Deck Four and stopped to wait for Maria, Michael and Jasmine to pass, swapping positions. The door in the side of the ship was huge. You could probably drive a car through it on a big enough ramp. Barker recognised it as the one he had entered through when he'd boarded all those days ago. The sunlight was blinding and the ship's air conditioning failed to stop the heat of the sun entering and beckoning them outside.

Barker's heart raced as he wondered whether this was the

point at which Rob and Maria would decide it was all over for them and dump them in the sea. There was a bright orange and white lifeboat tied up outside, blocking the view of the water and the horizon. A figure was moving around inside, but before Barker could see any more, Jasmine made her move. Seeing an opportunity, she stopped suddenly at the front of the line-up and jerked herself backwards into Michael, who let out a loud "Ooof!" and stumbled back towards Maria. Maria had left enough room to react but only if one of them made a move, not both. She couldn't deal with two of them and was unsighted now by Michael stumbling toward her. Jasmine meanwhile had reset herself and started sprinting for the door, attracted by the hope of freedom. She took four or five long strides and jumped up onto the right-hand side of the lifeboat, but sprung immediately off it into the sea below, diving like an Olympic swimmer, and disappeared.

Barker and Lucy saw most of what happened over Maria's shoulder and turned to each other.

"It's always the quiet ones," said Lucy.

Barker allowed himself to crack a tiny smile as he looked at Lucy and said, "Good for her", but as he turned to look back at the lifeboat his smile disappeared. The figure in the lifeboat emerged slowly and carefully into the daylight and down the steps onto Starlight's deck and looked up.

"Laura?" he whispered almost inaudibly as his vision dimmed and blurred and the blood left his face and dropped to his feet, followed immediately by his stomach. He began to lose control of his knees and this time Lucy had to take his weight properly to stop him from hitting the floor.

"John?!" Lucy mouthed in slow motion, but Barker didn't hear. He was trying to focus on the apparition he'd just seen

303

and when he did his heart bounced up through his throat as he looked over at the woman in front of him. His stomach gave up the fight and threw up its contents.

Chapter 108

"Hello John," said the woman who was supposed to be dead.

"How?...What?" Barker managed, wiping the mess from his mouth.

"Yes. Sorry."

"You...you died. I was away but Rob identified..." Barker's voice trailed off as the realisation hit him.

"I remember."

Barker turned around to look at Rob, who avoided his gaze and looked at Laura instead.

"You and Rob?"

"Yes John."

"How long?"

"John, we don't have to.."

"How long!" Barker shouted angrily.

"A year, maybe. On and off."

"On and...." Barker shut his eyes and swayed, "Why?"

"Really? Right now?" Laura said going from soft to stern in seconds. "I was sick of the life John. I never saw you. Marrying a policeman was a mistake. Even my job got dangerous, as you well know. I'd had enough."

"So you went off with another cop who works for the man who tried to have you killed?"

"He doesn't work for him John, they used each other. It's all about contacts. Anyway, Rob interrupted my attackers. He's the reason I didn't die. He said they'd probably be back if I didn't disappear. He promised me a way out."

"The baby...I thought you did it..."

"I *was* suicidal John. I wanted to die. If Rob hadn't taken me away..."

"So you ran off with him to work for that psychopath," Barker said, nodding at Michael, "who's been killing people for the last week and you thought that was an easier life?"

"Michael hasn't killed anybody John. He tried to make Maria disappear and failed – he's as bad at killing people as he is dealing drugs."

Michael grimaced, took a deep breath and shook his head from side to side, but said nothing.

"So who the hell did?" Lucy interrupted.

"Me," said Laura.

Barker and Lucy both froze, like they'd misheard something.

"You?!" said Barker in disbelief. "What?!"

"Or why?" said Lucy. "Why kill innocent people?"

"Because they tried to kill me," Laura added. "They beat the crap out of me and left me for dead. You can still see the scars." Laura pointed at a mark running diagonally across her right cheek that Lucy hadn't noticed before. "There are worse ones under my clothes. Especially where they took out my dead babies." Lucy looked away.

"Babies?!" said Barker.

"Yes John. Twins. You were never available for the scans remember? So I thought I'd keep it as a surprise."

"The people here didn't attack you," said Lucy, changing the subject and holding onto Barker who was wobbling even more.

"They might as well have done," said Laura, "They're all the same, all part of the same dirty organisation. I wanted them to feel my pain. And it served a purpose in hurrying Michael up. We knew he was going to ransom them and the ship, but we thought if Savenas Seaways's family started dropping like flies it would focus his attention."

"You're sick."

"Maybe, but a share of twenty million will make me better. And I didn't kill all of them myself. I had help."

Barker and Lucy turned towards Maria. "That one I know about," Barker said.

"Look, this is very nice but we have a schedule to keep so can we get out of here now?" Maria interrupted. "There are people waiting for us."

"Maria's right," Rob said, "We're all caught up now so let's move. Get in the boat." Rob pointed at the waiting lifeboat that Laura had stepped out of and gestured for Barker and Lucy to carry on walking towards it.

Chapter 109

Barker turned to look at Lucy and held her wrist with his right hand and gently pulled his left hand out of her grip. At first she looked puzzled but her expression slowly changed to fear as she realised what this meant. Barker's face was calm. He was no longer conflicted. He knew what he had to do and Lucy was just about to find out. Barker had a new sense of purpose and gathered a reserve of energy from deep down, maybe it was his last. But he knew it had to be done. He mouthed the word "Sorry" at Lucy and, for the second time that day, launched himself at someone.

Rob was momentarily off guard, caught between looking protectively at Laura, and the lifeboat which was their route to a new life with their share of Maria's recently-stolen money. He just saw Barker move and began to aim his gun before there was any contact. But he didn't manage to squeeze the trigger before he was flattened by ninety kilos of pissed-off widower/ex-husband and slammed to the floor. The gun fell out of his hand and scudded across the carpet.

Michael saw his chance and jumped over them both, ignoring his bleeding shoulder, and picked up the gun. Instinctively he pointed it at the nearest person, who happened to be Lucy. They locked eyes silently for a couple of seconds until Michael decided she wasn't a threat and his best option was to head for the door. He turned towards the lifeboat only to see Maria spinning round and assessing the situation, raising her own weapon and preparing to fire. Michael did the same but noticed a change in her expression as she changed her aim to somewhere over his shoulder.

But Maria didn't need to shoot anyone. Down the corridor they were stood in, that spanned the ship's width, came a large male figure at full speed, heading straight for Michael. Sam and Jordan had caught up with Barker and Lucy and had followed events from the opposite end of the corridor, waiting for an opportunity. This was it. Jordan clattered into the back of Michael. Maria didn't need to worry about Michael anymore. She just had to take advantage of her own opportunity to escape the chaos. She turned towards the lifeboat and saw Laura's panicked expression.

"Get on the boat!" Maria shouted.

"But...Rob!" Laura protested.

"But nothing!" Maria replied, "Get on the boat!"

Lucy watched Jordan and Michael hit the ground, then turned and looked at Barker, who had managed to land one good blow to the side of Rob's head and was flailing around trying to finish the job but using up all his energy. Rob was bigger and more athletic and hadn't already been in a fight that morning so was able to flip Barker over and pin him down. Out of the corner of her eye, Lucy saw Michael's gun bounce out of his hand and across the corridor again, but it was too far away to get to before Rob did some damage to Barker. She had to act now.

Rob sat more upright as Barker tried in vain to lift him off or free his hands to attack him again. His energy was depleting so fast as he struggled to regain the advantage. This was the struggle of a man prepared to die for something, but likely to be a fight he couldn't win.

"You should have stayed out of it John. It didn't have to come to this," Rob said.

Barker pulled his left hand free and swung wildly at the right side of Rob's head, clipping his jaw. Rob grimaced and pulled back his right arm to land a blow on Barker that would knock him out cold if not finish him off. But just as he was about to let go of his right fist, a loud metallic thud on the back of his head sent him face down on top of Barker. Lucy had pulled a fire extinguisher off the wall and swung it at him. She dropped it straight away, kneeled down, and rolled Rob's lifeless body off Barker's exhausted one.

"John? John? Are you OK?" she asked Barker, who slumped flat on his back and took the first of several deep breaths to recover from what could have been his last fight.

"Mmmm" he murmured, unable to speak at first. "Think so."

Jordan had less trouble with Michael. He had noticed his bullet-wounded arm and twisted it behind Michael's back, whilst pinning him face-down on the blood-stained carpet. His wife Sam had come out of hiding and sat on Michael's legs to help take him out of the fight.

Barker looked in the direction of the door at the lifeboat that was edging away from the side of Starlight. He could see Laura looking through a window in the side of the boat. Was she looking at him, or looking for Rob? Either way her future was not going to turn out as she'd planned. Barker felt nothing for her now. He had lost her six months ago and after the shock of seeing her again and learning what she and Rob had done to him, it was easy now to close that chapter.

Maria appeared at the door of the boat as it gathered speed and headed away from the ship, and raised her gun in its direction. Lucy remembered the gun Michael had dropped and jumped up and across the corridor to grab it. "No, Lucy, No!" Barker shouted.

Lucy got to the gun in time and picked it up, but didn't get chance to even aim it before Barker heard a crack from the lifeboat. Lucy dropped onto the floor.

Chapter 110

Maria disappeared into the lifeboat as it sped away towards the shore in the glorious Caribbean sunshine and perfect blue sea. Michael gave up resisting the two people sat on top of him having run out of energy and, almost, blood. Barker pulled himself up with what energy he had left and scrambled over to where Lucy lay on her right side, adding to the blood on the luxurious carpet. He moved around and kneeled in front of her and put his hand on her left shoulder.

"Lucy! Are you OK?" he asked desperately.

After a couple of seconds, Lucy said, "I've got a hole in my leg, what do *you* think?"

Barker looked across and saw her dress stuck to the entry wound on the outside of her left thigh with blood trickling out.

"It's just a flesh wound."

"Piss off."

"No, I mean it's not hit an artery. That would have been nasty."

"This isn't exactly a bowl of cherries but I'll survive. Won't I?"

Barker nodded and smiled at Lucy properly for the first time that day, with a relief he hadn't felt since he'd boarded the ship, or maybe even since before Laura left. This felt like a proper ending. And maybe a new beginning. He rolled Lucy over gently onto her back, went round to lift her shoulders and sat her up against the wall behind her, then began to take off his shirt.

"John, this isn't the time or place," Lucy said, deadpan, grimacing with pain.

"It's for pressure on the wound OK? Apologies for having to look at my flabby white chest for a bit until we get you seen by a doctor."

"It's the best offer I'm going to get today," Lucy said with a hint of a smile.

"I think you're going to be OK," John replied.

Chapter 111

It worked. I got them back for what they did, and I got my new life. It didn't all go to plan though. I lost my man. Again. But he was just a means to an end. And the old one seems to have moved on without me. She's young and pretty. Maybe they'll have kids. Wouldn't that be ironic?

Now I just have to work out if I want to share this money with my accomplice. It's in her bank so I guess I need to keep her around for now. She's a tough one though. Not worth the fight. Maybe I'll just take ten million and run.

Chapter 112

"The medical centre is just through there," said Sam pointing at one of the crew doors off the main corridor where all the action had happened.

"Are you a doctor?" Barker replied.

"I'm a veterinary nurse, but I can find some painkillers and dress that wound properly so you can put your shirt back on."

"Bit late now, it's covered in blood."

"I can think of another use for it," Jordan added. "Tie this guy's arms together behind his back and we'll *all* go to the sickbay."

"I'm not going anywhere with him." Lucy interrupted, "He's the reason we're all in this mess."

Barker took the shirt that he'd started to wrap around Lucy's leg and walked over to Sam and handed it over. Sam pulled Michael's wrists together and used the shirtsleeves to tie them together tightly. Then she stood and helped Barker to lift Lucy onto her feet. Barker took the weight on her injured side while Lucy hopped and Sam supported her on her right side.

The medical centre was only a few metres down the corridor. The door was unlocked.

"Must've left in a hurry like everyone else," Sam said.

"Medical centre's a grand title for three beds and a desk isn't it?" said Lucy.

"If it's got drugs and bandages it'll do."

Barker sat Lucy down on the edge of the bed and lifted her legs as she twisted sideways onto the plastic-covered bench which was raised at one end. He arranged a couple of pillows behind her head so she could lie down. Sam opened some cupboards and found dressings and came over to put them on Lucy's wound.

"Put this on top of her leg and hold firmly down until I come back. I'll be back in a minute when I've taken these other dressings to Jordan."

Barker lifted Lucy's dress where it was stuck to the blood around the bullet hole on the outside of her left thigh, halfway between her hip and her knee.

"Don't get any ideas," said Lucy "You've only taken me out for dinner once."

Barker ignored her and gently put the dressing over the centre of the wound and pressed down. Lucy winced and breathed in sharply as she fought back tears.

"I'm sorry," said Barker.

"What for?" said Lucy, "You didn't shoot me."

"For getting you into this."

"It's not like you dragged me along with you John."

"If I hadn't spilled that drink over you..."

"Because you were staring at a gorgeous woman in a slinky swimsuit climbing out of the pool?" Lucy interrupted.

Barker laughed, "If I hadn't spilled..."

"The gorgeous woman that just shot me?"

"You'd never have got involved."

"Yes I would John. My father owns the company that Michael was holding to ransom. Michael would probably still have kidnapped me and used me but you'd never have known and been my knight in shining armour."

"Knights don't tend to get their victims shot though do they?"

"They don't tend to lose a fight and need rescuing themselves either, but here we are."

Lucy put her hand on top of the hand Barker was holding the dressing with and they looked at each other.

"It's me that should be sorry," said Lucy.

"Why?"

"That gorgeous bitch got away with twenty million. That would have come in really useful right now. I think I'm out of a job."

"You won't be out of work for long."

"I won't be strutting my stuff on stage for a while."

"Oh yeah. Hadn't thought of that," Barker looked down at Lucy's leg.

"She didn't get a penny," said a voice from the entrance as the door swung gently open.

"Marcus!" said Lucy "You scared me half to death. I'd forgotten about you."

"Most people do," Marcus replied.

"I mean... I'm sorry. Are you OK? What do you mean?"

Marcus walked into the room properly and sat down in a chair by another of the beds.

"You did it?" Barker asked.

"Easy. Although I barely had enough time."

"Will someone tell me what's going on please?!" Lucy demanded.

"You tell her. I'm still getting my breath back after running around trying to find you all."

Barker laughed to himself and turned back to Lucy.

"You remember when I sent you to that room and stayed back with Marcus?"

"Uh huh."

"Well I knew the moment I first saw him in the meeting room that he was a computer geek."

"None taken," Marcus interrupted.

"Sorry Marcus but it...it's the T-shirts. Dead giveaway."

"I have no dress sense."

"Anyway," Barker continued, "having seen what Michael, then Maria, was trying to do, I thought Marcus might be able to stop them. Sounds like he did."

"I logged on to the ship's intranet and found the PC they were using in the Adriatic suite and was able to take over control just in time to change the details they'd entered."

"Which means what? What details?" Lucy asked.

"The account details. The money didn't go to Maria's bank account."

"Which one did it go to?"

"The only one I know by heart," Barker said, "Mine."

Lucy's mouth opened and it took a few seconds for her to say, "Shit John! You mean you're twenty million more attractive than when I first met you?"

"I think so."

"So why were you saying sorry again?"

"Well I don't think I'm going to hang onto it."

Lucy raised an eyebrow.

"It's not my money, is it? I was just diverting it away from the criminals. Besides, I can think of a few charities that would be very grateful for an anonymous boost in their finances."

Lucy looked deflated. "You know how to disappoint a girl

John. I was just planning on recuperating in the Caribbean for a few weeks...or years."

"Well I'm sure we can deduct a few expenses first," Barker said with a smile.

"I'm going to need a new wardrobe."

"Me too...apparently," added Marcus.

XII

DAY NINETEEN: NASSAU

Chapter 113

A week after leaving Galaxy Starlight behind on the Pilot boat that was the first to arrive to check for people left behind, Barker walked down the corridor of the Princess Margaret Hospital on Shirley Street in Nassau, to the room where Lucy was recovering. The doctors had found no bullet so had cleaned and stitched her wounds and insisted she get some rest. Today she would be allowed to leave, as long as she returned for a check-up in a few days time before leaving the island. When Barker entered the room Lucy was sat on the edge of the bed waiting, bags packed.

"Someone's keen," he said, smiling.

Lucy smiled back and stood up with her weight on her good leg and gathered the metal crutches she'd been given.

"No need. I've arranged a wheelchair to get you down to the entrance."

"I'm walking out of here under my own steam John," Lucy said with a stern look.

"OK," Barker put his hands up in submission. "I was just trying to help."

"I know, but I've been sat up in bed for nearly a week apart from a few physio sessions. I've got to move."

"Fine. Let me carry your bag."

"Thank you for upgrading my room. The ward wasn't great"

"Least I could do, under the circumstances."

Barker grabbed Lucy's bags after helping her with her crutches and waited until she started moving towards the door. They made slow progress to the nearest lift and waited for a ride down three floors to reception.

Outside the front of the building a white taxi was waiting. Lucy moved to one side to let other people come past her whilst Barker loaded her bags into the trunk and came back for her. He opened the back door, took her crutches, and helped her sit down inside.

"Not going to be that easy getting out," Lucy said.

"We'll manage," replied Barker as he climbed in next to her from the other side.

"How far is the hotel?"

"About ten minutes."

"I thought you said you'd been staying close by?"

"I did while you were in here, but it was a bit basic. OK for me on my own but I thought you deserved a bit of luxury. We can afford it."

The taxi pulled away from the hospital entrance and headed into the town centre.

About eight minutes later the car pulled up outside the Rosewood Baha Mar hotel. Lucy stared out of the window, smiled, and turned back to Barker, "Bet this is expensive."

"No idea, I haven't booked yet. But the hotel I was in before said it would be quiet – too expensive for your average tourist, and all Starlight's passengers have been repatriated now. And it's still early season. We might have it to ourselves."

A doorman appeared and opened Lucy's door and held out his hand, "Allow me."

Barker jumped out of his door, said "I'll get the crutches," and ran to the trunk. Another man had already opened it and was loading the bags onto a trolley to take inside.

Lucy grabbed the crutches and straightened up as she began to walk towards the door, with the doorman opening it for her and Barker following. The reception inside was all white marble, tropical plants and handmade wooden furniture. Barker noticed the reception desk and headed over. One of the young women behind the desk greeted him as he turned to make sure Lucy was next to him.

"Good afternoon Sir, how can I help?" said the young lady.

"I believe the Towne Hotel enquired about availability for me this morning. I'd like to book two rooms for three nights please."

"OK sir, I'm sure that won't be a..."

"*One* room." Lucy interrupted and said to the receptionist. "One room is fine thanks."

Barker turned to look at Lucy who raised an eyebrow and smiled. He caught his breath for a second and turned back, "One room please."

Chapter 114

Outside in a side street facing the hotel, another white taxi sat idling in the warm morning air. In the back seat sat a tall, olive-skinned woman with long black hair tied in a ponytail wearing a white linen dress, a floppy wide-brimmed hat and expensive sunglasses, clutching a large straw handbag. She leaned forward, handed some cash over the driver's shoulder, and in a soft South American accent, said, "I'll get out here, thank you."

About the Author

You can connect with me on:
🌐 https://www.stevenlea.com
📘 https://www.facebook.com/stevenleaauthor

Subscribe to my newsletter:
✉ https://www.stevenlea.com

Printed in Great Britain
by Amazon